wild

RECKLESS MC OPEY TEXAS CHAPTER

WALL STREET JOURNAL & USA TODAY BESTSELLING AUTHOR

KB WINTERS

Copyright and Disclaimer

This book is a work of fiction. The names, characters, places and incidents are products of the writer's imagination and have been used fictitiously and are not to be construed as real. Any resemblance to persons, living or dead, actual events, locales or organizations is entirely coincidental.

Copyright © 2020 Book Boyfriends Publishing

All rights reserved. No part of this publication may be reproduced, stored in or introduced into a retrieval system, or transmitted, in any form, or by any means (electronic, mechanical, photocopying, recording, or otherwise) without the prior written permission of the copyright owner. The author acknowledges the trademarked status and trademark owners of various products referenced in this work of fiction, which have been used without permission. The publication/use of the trademarks is not authorized, associated with, or sponsored by the trademark owners.

Table of Contents

Copyright and Disclaimer ii
Chapter One 7
Chapter Two 15
Chapter Three 23
Chapter Four 33
Chapter Five 45
Chapter Six 55
Chapter Seven 63
Chapter Eight 71
Chapter Nine 83
Chapter Ten 91
Chapter Eleven 101
Chapter Twelve 109
Chapter Thirteen 121
Chapter Fourteen 131
Chapter Fifteen 143
Chapter Sixteen 149
Chapter Seventeen 159
Chapter Eighteen 165
Chapter Nineteen 171
Chapter Twenty 179
Chapter Twenty-One 189

Chapter Twenty-Two	197
Chapter Twenty-Three	209
Chapter Twenty-Four	221
Chapter Twenty-Five	233
Chapter Twenty-Six	247
Chapter Twenty-Seven	257
Chapter Twenty-Eight	269
Chapter Twenty-Nine	281
Chapter Thirty	293
Chapter Thirty-One	301
Chapter Thirty-Two	311
Chapter Thirty-Three	321
Chapter Thirty-Four	329
Chapter Thirty-Five	333
Epilogue	341

WILD

Reckless MC Opey Texas Chapter Book 6

By Wall Street Journal & USA Today Bestselling Author

KB Winters

Chapter One

Slayer

Boring as fuck. Those were the three words that came to mind a lot lately. I never thought I'd say that after becoming a member of the Reckless Bastards. The truth was that things were boring more often than not, despite all the secret CIA fucking feds, crazy boyfriends with ties to gangs, mobsters and all the other bullshit the MC had been through over the past seven years I'd been here at the ranch. *Damn! Hs it been that long?* I lost track when shit was popping, but when it wasn't…it was boring as fuck.

As fuck.

Even now, sitting thirty feet from a room filled with half-naked people in The Barn Door, looking for a good, hard fuck, I was bored. If I was in there *and* not on the clock, I'd be having fun at least. Instead, I was out here working the door as punishment even though Gunnar said it wasn't punishment. He gave me some bullshit story that our prospect Ford, needed some experience working inside the club. That was bullshit, and we both knew it, but I didn't mind because when shit was boring it didn't matter where you were bored.

Boredom was flexible like that.

Who knew bein' in an MC would be just as monotonous as the service? I mean, it was the exact same kind of hurry up and wait bullshit before you got to see any action. Some of the guys hated the action, figured it was a good damn day if they didn't have to pull a trigger or spill blood. Not me. I thrived on the action. It was where I felt most alive. I was nobody's adrenaline junkie but growing up in chaos made it real easy to get used to it. The government found they could take that, shape it, and turn me into something useful. Lethal.

And Goddamnit, I was getting old.

But at least, I wasn't throwing punches at an enemy or lining up a shot on some terrorist. Hell I wasn't even knee-deep in pussy. I was a glorified fucking doorman at a sex club. Okay, a sex club where I was part owner, but still. Gunnar didn't play that owner shit. He cleaned up come and puke and other bodily fluids and expected the rest of us to do the same. And tonight, that meant door duty.

I didn't know how the fuck Ford could sit here for hours upon hours, doing jack shit in this little box that was about ten feet by eight feet. Maybe it was because he was always on that fucking computer of his, but I wasn't a techy kind of guy so I didn't have that, and I was going out of my fucking mind. So much so that I guess I must have dozed off.

"What the fuck?" I said when a sharp smack on the back of my head woke me up really quick.

Gunnar's angry blue eyes glared down at me hard enough that he would've melted a lesser man. "Having a nice nap?"

I sat up and stretched my upper body, muscle by muscle, smiling up at my glowering Prez. "It was more of a catnap, but it was all right. What's up?"

"What's up? Seriously Slayer?"

He crossed his big ass biceps over his chest, making him look like a big angry gorilla.

"What the fuck is up is that tonight, *you* are our first line of fucking defense. And sleeping, you're no fucking defense at all."

He was right. I sat up straight and said, "I hear ya." I had no fucking excuse for sleeping on the job. No amount of boredom was an excuse for risking your brothers' safety. "Really, Gunnar, I hear ya."

"Good," he growled. "Because if someone else paints these fucking walls with his brains, yours are goin' right beside him. I mean it."

The expression on his face was ice cold. Stony. I knew this was more than just run of the mill worrying.

"I said I hear you, Gunnar. What's going on?" He was a worrier by nature, our Prez. You couldn't grow up the way he had and not worry all the fucking time. Sometimes his big burly ass was even a mother hen, but right now he was scared. "Gunnar?"

"Nothing really, not yet anyway. But I need to know I can count on all of you right now."

"My bad, Gunnar. I have no fucking excuse man. I'm sorry, but you can always fucking count on me."

"Good. Just keep your eyes peeled, and if you notice anything or anyone that gives you a bad feeling, I wanna know about it."

Shit. Something was going on with the Prez, and he didn't want us to know about it, not yet anyway. I nodded. "You got it, bro."

"Thanks." He nodded and took my words at face value, arms still crossed. He got lost in his thoughts, and I let him. Gunnar clearly had a lot on his mind, and the best thing I could do was give him one less thing to worry about.

He pointed to the door. "Go inside and do a circuit of the place. Flirt with a few girls and come back ready to finish out the night right here. Ya hear me, Slayer?"

I was already on my feet with a wide, grateful smile. "Thanks, man. You need to talk, I'm here."

Gunnar laughed. "Yeah? You want to talk about why Stone keeps waking up at four in the morning for no damn reason?"

Not particularly. "If that's what you need to talk about." His kid was cute as fuck, and I enjoyed spending time with the little dude, but talking about kids sounded boring as fuck.

"Thanks, but no thanks, Slayer. I'll talk when I'm ready." And not a moment before, we all knew that, but the offer always stood.

"Then I'll go break a few hearts and come back to relieve you."

"Just flirt, Slayer. Don't leave me out here while you're off getting your dick wet."

My smile brightened. "Wouldn't dream of it." Turning away with one hand on the knob, waiting for Gunnar to press the button that would allow me entry into The Barn Door, I could already feel the pulsing beat of the music on the other side. Ever since Cruz and his chick, Hennessy, put on that big ass party a few months back, Gunnar'd been happy to keep up running themes one night a week. It brought in newcomers, which always brought in more money. That was good for the MC.

Tonight, the whole place looked like a Greek orgy, or what one would have looked like if it had thrown up. Gold and white was everywhere, along with olive branches and leaves, big ass chalices and trays with fruits and cheeses were everywhere. It was actually pretty great, and I'd tell Hennessy, but not Cruz. That fucker would let it go to his head. Especially because, true to form, the regulars were all dressed according to the theme.

Only these were rich ass Texans, not broke ass college kids like the one toga party I went to on leave. The women here were wrapped in white silk that barely covered their tits and gave tempting glimpses of pussy lips and all the ways women loved to adorn their pussies. Gold cuffs and gems were everywhere, but I didn't give a fuck about that, my eyes ate up all the flesh on display.

And that's when I see *her*. A tall blonde with the sweetest pair of dick-sucking lips I'd ever seen was bopping her head to the beat. Alone. She was hot as fuck, at least an eight from where I stood, but these idiots were either too scared or too stupid to make her feel welcome.

I wasn't stupid and I didn't do scared, so I flashed a smile and ran a hand through my long brown hair and walked over to her with a smile on my face. "Gold is definitely your color, sweetheart."

Surprise lit in baby blue eyes that were, unfortunately dilated all to fuck. She smiled and offered her hand. "Thanks. Audrey."

"Slayer." I took her hand in mine, disappointed the stacked blonde was too high to take to bed tonight. "You all right, Audrey?"

She shrugged and giggled, then stumbled. "I'm good. These shoes are killing me."

"Take'em off. In that dress, no one will notice." She smiled again and when her skin flushed pink, I felt a rush of masculine pride go through me and stepped closer. Just because I couldn't fuck her tonight didn't mean I couldn't flirt with her.

"Charmer," she murmured, biting her bottom lip. "I bet you've got a big cock too."

Yep, she was definitely on something. "Any other night that's a bet I'm willing to take, Audrey, but you're fucked up."

She giggled and pressed those DD tits against my chest. I could feel her hard nipples poking through the silky gold fabric, and fuck me, I was tempted. I was more than tempted when her hand wrapped around my cock through my jeans and squeezed. "I just wanna get fucked. By you. That's all."

My cock hardened in her hand and she licked her lips, those dick-sucking lips that only made me harder imagining her on her knees in front of me, taking my cock down her throat. But she was high, and I liked my women fully engaged.

"Not tonight," I told her and waved at Saint who was slinging drinks behind the bar. She needed water. And a chaperone.

"Let me get you a drink."

That got her moving easily, and as soon as Hazel set a bottle of water in front of her, I took off to finish my circuit, suddenly eager to get back to my little box of boredom.

Chapter Two

Ella Mae

"All right, we're done. Now get the fuck outta here." That was Curtis Reeves, one of my closest friends and the President of my MC, the Lords of Buckthorn. He was a tough son of a bitch, but he didn't stand on ceremony, not even when it came to something as small as ending a club meeting.

The other Lords stood and filtered out of our temporary meeting place, while our club house was being put back together. After a particularly nasty fight with a group of Mexican gun runners, the club house had suffered fire and water damage.

"It'll be nice to get back to the Lair," I said.

The Lords' Lair was where we held church. We discussed all club business inside the Lair, and every time we met here, it made me want to kill those gun runners all over again.

Curt laughed and shook his head, lighting up a joint laced with tobacco as soon as we were out in the warm Texas sunshine.

"Thanks to you puttin' the fear of God in those contractors, Ella, should be meeting there again this time next week." He took a long pull on his hand-rolled cigarette and let it out with a satisfied exhale.

"It'll be nice to put the table back where he belongs."

The *he* Curt referred to was the original Lord, Carter Buckthorn, whose shoulder-length, feathered brown hair and thick handlebar moustache were carved into the table. Two sapphires stood in for his eyes, and his handlebars were etched in chrome on the table with him. Forever. It was as sacred as church for us, more so because we actually fuckin' meant it.

"I'll bring the booze to re-christen the room."

Curt flashed another smile at me and took another pull on the cigarette, staring off in the distance the way he did when he had something on his mind. It could be anything, and as his second in command, and the first female Veep of any MC in Texas, I learned early on not to guess. Curt would reveal himself in his own time so I slid my sunglasses over my eyes and leaned against the wooden fence outside the club that separated the grassy area from the graveled makeshift parking lot.

"We've had a lot of shit to deal with lately."

"We have," I agreed, shit like the bullet wound in my thigh that had finally faded to almost invisible, or the stab wound in my side that had only been healed for a few months.

"Between the Irish mob and the cartels, we've lost three men. The Bratva isn't much better, but at least we expect constant bullshit from them." They had access to quality guns and those fuckers knew it, constantly changing terms, meeting places and all other types of shenanigans.

"But right now, our biggest problem is Leon, and that's a big fucking problem for me, Chance."

Curt used my biker name, Chance, when he discussed club business. I nodded, knowing he was right, but also knew that Leon was harmless. "You did what you had to do."

Leon used to be a part of our MC, but his own behavior got him kicked out, a fact he took with surprising calm. Our breakup? Not so much.

"I know. So did you. But Leon is becoming a problem, Chance, and if you don't deal with him, I will." It was more of a promise than a threat, but there was no doubt about what he meant.

"I'll take care of him," I said without looking up. It was a foolish promise, one I wasn't sure I could keep.

But I hoped Leon's sense of self-preservation mattered more to him than us getting back together, because that would never fucking happen. Ever.

"Good," Curt said, a warning in his usually friendly voice. "I'll see you later."

Curt walked towards his bike parked about six feet from the door of our temporary space. It was an old utility shed on the south side of Buckthorn Farm that we rented from one of Carter's great-grandchildren. I'd parked my bike in a gravel covered lot that was more dust than anything, the spot all the other Lords used.

My blue and chrome Harley sat there all alone, gleaming in the sunlight, and I couldn't help but smile. My love of motorcycles, the only thing I ever got from my piece of shit father, had ended up being the thing that had saved my life. Had given me purpose. And power. And that had made me stronger, tougher and more confident. Kicking Leon to the curb and becoming VP of my MC had only made me...*more*.

***

Before I had time to strap on my helmet, I heard a familiar voice behind me.

"Looking gorgeous today, Ella."

It would have been a nice change if it was a surprise to see Leon, but the stupid fucker showed up every day. Wherever I was, he managed to find me and show up to plead his case.

He stood between me and the road out of the parking lot, but as usual, I ignored him. As a woman in the twenty-first century, I was used to little boys not being able to handle rejection, but Leon took it to new heights.

"You're not even gonna acknowledge me?"

I turned to face Leon, mostly because I didn't trust his unstable ass, but also because this man used to matter to me. He used to be my whole world and now, when I stared at his blond hair and green eyes, those boy-next-door looks, all I felt was annoyance. And anger. There was no leftover love and no breakup goggles. I made the right decision and every time I saw him only proved it. "Why should I say anything when you clearly have a hearing problem?"

"Maybe if you were saying what I wanted to hear, I'd listen." He tried for a smile, but these days he looked more gaunt than jacked, more crackhead chic than biker sexy.

"Ella, baby cakes." He reached for me, and I took a step back and got in a fighting stance. He wouldn't catch me off guard.

Not again.

"Just listen to me, Ella. We were good together and if you'd just listen—"

"No. I'm done listening to you, Leon. I suggest you get the fuck out of Oakley, hell, get the fuck out of Texas, if you know what's good for you."

It wasn't the first time I issued that warning, but that glazed look in his eyes said it did about as much good this time as it had the previous one hundred times.

He smiled and pulled himself up a little taller, but that crazed look hadn't left his eyes, so I kept my guard all the way up.

"That's a good idea. We could leave Texas, start over somewhere away from all this MC bullshit."

I barked out a bitter laugh. "MC bullshit? I seem to recall you used to live for this *bullshit*."

Leon used to bleed Lords of Buckthorn MC, until he lost his fucking mind. Apparently, he still hadn't found it.

"You need to stop this Leon. There will never be a me and you again. You made sure of it."

Not only could I *not* date a former Buckthorn MC member even if I wanted to, but he put hands on me and that shit is an immediate deal breaker.

"Be reasonable, Ella."

"I am." I grabbed my helmet and slid it down over my head with the windscreen open and straddled my bike. "You might want to consider making better choices than the ones that got you kicked out in the first place." I didn't need to wait for Leon to say anything else because I'd heard it all before, most of it over the past four months.

He was relentless and just a little bit crazy, but Leon wasn't a danger to anyone but himself. And that's what made it easy to start my bike and ride away, leaving him with nothing more than a big ass cloud of dust to hang on to, because that was all I'd ever give him.

Between the headache that was Leon and all the shit the MC had to deal with lately, I hadn't even had a proper orgasm in a good few months. The rest of the guys, at least, had the Ladies of Buckthorn to choose from when they needed a therapeutic fuck session to keep from going crazy. When I needed a good hard plow, I had to go out and find it.

And that's exactly what I planned to do tonight.

Get drunk and get fucked. If that failed, hopefully, I'd get to kick some ass.

Chapter Three

Slayer

"You sure you don't wanna hang?" Cruz looked up at me with those creepy ass blue eyes of his, an amused smirk on his face as he asked the question.

"Yeah," I snorted. "I'm sure."

I loved my brothers, even most of their women were cool too, but there was no fucking way in hell I was spending a free night with them. "I'll pass on the board game but you have fun on my behalf."

Cruz shook his head and ran a hand through his dirty blond hair, that damn smirk still on his face.

"Where you headed off to tonight, just in case you need a ride. Or bail."

"One goddamn time and you won't stop bringing it up." In all fairness, I wouldn't either if I was in his shoes, but I didn't need to be reminded of that particular night right now. "I don't know, probably heading to someplace *not* in Opey."

"Sick of the busybodies all up in your business?"

The old ladies in Opey were more than a handful and for some reason they loved me. "Nope, just in the mood for something new tonight." Something other than women looking to get off with a cowboy or a biker, and definitely not someone I'm likely to run into when I go into town for a beer. Or groceries.

"Have fun. Be safe."

"And don't do anything I wouldn't," Hennessy said as she came up behind Cruz and wrapped her arms around him. "Or anything he wouldn't."

I cocked an eyebrow at his little redheaded wife who had enough attitude for twenty women. "Lately? That means the world is my oyster."

"Yeah? You wanna hear about this thing Cruz does with his tongue? He sticks it—"

"I stopped listening after 'yeah'," I told her and she laughed.

"Good luck tonight, Slayer. Be safe."

"Thanks. You too." I took my time walking away from the main house, inhaling the sweet scent of flowers blooming in the air. I kind of hated that I knew shit like that but living in Texas and working the land made folks appreciate the simple beauty of nature.

WILD

The ride out of Opey was empty even though it was only ten o'clock. Most of the people in the area kept farmer's hours except for all the ranch hands who kept all the bars in the area in business.

Tonight I made my way out to Rusty Hinges, a dirt road bar on a tiny half-mile strip of land that was neither Opey nor Oakley. A small strip of lawless land, perfect to find a hot piece for the night. Inside, the place was already rowdy and the music had switched from good ol' boy country to rock. In another hour the jukebox would start playing heavy metal and the fights would start.

I hoped to be wrapped around a woman with long legs well before then.

I walked up to the bar and said, "A beer. Something dark and on tap," to the bartender, a cute little blonde with a righteous set of tits.

A pearl snap shirt held them snugly in place and her blue jeans made her ass look like a question mark from the right angle.

"Coming right up. Tab?" she asked.

"Nah, I'll pay as I go. Add a double shot of Patron to that, too, will ya? Thanks."

She headed to the end of the bar to get my drinks, and I turned to scan the packed crowd, looking to see if there was anyone here worth making an effort for. So far it was the same old crowd of women with big hair, pink lips and that sexy cowgirl chic look that I'd seen a thousand times. Fucked a hundred times. And grew bored of at least thirty fucks ago.

That's when I saw her, looking like a sexy badass in a leather jacket. Not one of those bullshit pleather jackets meant for fashion, this shit had a heavy-duty zipper and enough pockets to carry what you needed for a smooth, clean getaway.

She had dark brown hair that had strands of blonde that gleamed when she moved under the different lights. Her hair hung down her back and brushed against her tits in the front, a feature that stole all of my attention as she made her way to the bar.

Beneath the jacket she wore a small leather handkerchief that showed off a slim waist and hips perfect for grabbing on to. She came to a stop at the empty spot next to me at the bar, smelling like leather and vanilla, the scent of coconuts and cigarettes wafting from her hair, and when her gaze swung to mine, those brown eyes softened the edges of her high cheekbones and sharp jawline.

"Like what you see cowboy?"

I arched a brow and leaned in to her. "If I look like a cowboy to you then you need those pretty little eyes checked."

Heat sparked in her eyes, but a moment later she barked out a laugh and shook her head. "No thanks. Next!"

Oh, she was feisty too. Nothing got my cock harder than a hot bitch who was feisty to boot.

The bartender returned with my drinks, and I pulled out my wallet. Without looking up from digging out a Franklin to pay my tab, I said, "Looking for a little boy you can control? I get that."

I shrugged and tossed back the shot of Patron, slamming the glass on the bar hard. I grabbed my beer and took a swig, looking out at the crowd for my second-round pick.

"Have a good night." I gave her a polite tip of my non-existent Stetson and walked around the makeshift dance floor where a few drunk souls tried to line dance to the rock blaring from the jukebox speakers.

I made a circle around the bar in search of another woman who caught my eye, one like that sexy ass brunette with the shitty attitude. She was hot and just my type, tall and curvy and knew she looked best in leather and denim, plus that sass. But I didn't beg, and

I sure as hell didn't do high maintenance. Despite her bad girl outer shell, she was definitely high maintenance.

Too bad for her.

I drank my beer and watched the women who danced together, gyrating against one another in an attempt to draw more male attention. I was beyond that, not beyond threesomes, just women who needed to advertise it. They were hot enough, but there wasn't one twitch behind my zipper. Unfortunately.

I refused to get hung up on any woman so I stood taller and looked around, smoothing out the frown on my face so I didn't scare off any of my potential fuck buddies.

"You think you got me all figured out, don't you? Well I know ten guys like you, and they all think they're some kind of genius."

I buried my smiling face in my beer as the hot brunette stood beside me, stewing between sips of her beer.

"I don't even know you, how could I have you figured out?" I wanted to figure her out, at least for the night.

WILD

"Oh please. You baited me and you know it. *Guess you prefer a little boy you can control,*" she mocked the deep timber of my voice. "It worked so don't go acting coy now."

I turned to her and took a step closer, appreciating the way her gaze lit with heat. Arousal. "Why'd you blow me off back there?"

"Hurt your ego?" The way those red lips curved woke my cock up as my mind conjured up images of that red lipstick ring where it belonged, around my cock.

"Fuck no. I saw the heat in your eyes, sweetheart. You want me. I just want to know what kind of games you're into before I decide if I wanna play."

The short denim skirt she wore made my fingers twitch to touch that soft skin of her inner thigh, to slide up higher to see if she was as wet as I thought she was.

"I don't play games."

"Then spill it, sugar."

She rolled her eyes and took a long, fortifying sip from her brown bottle. "You seem like trouble."

"You like trouble." The flare of heat in her gaze and the quickening of her pulse said I was right.

"I shouldn't."

"But you do, and I'm exactly the trouble you need tonight. I promise." This chick was hot as fuck and she gave good flirt. I was already sold.

"That's a bold promise when you don't know what I need." She finished off her beer and set the bottle on a table behind us.

"You look like you need a good, long, hard...*ride*."

Her breath hitched at the last word and then she let out a laugh that was sexy and husky, exactly what I hoped she sounded like when she came all over my cock. "Thought you weren't a cowboy?"

"Did I say that?" My adrenaline was pumping, the way it did when shit just clicked with a chick and the chub in my pants was ready to act as soon as she gave the greenlight.

"You did. Was that a lie?"

"I never lie to a pretty girl."

She arched a brow and put one hand on her hip, giving me a closer look at that leather handkerchief and the side boob I caught a quick glimpse of which made my mouth water.

"Do I look like a girl to you?"

"You look like all woman to me, which works out perfectly."

"Yeah?" She took a step closer and put her hands on my shoulders before she leaned in and whispered, "Why?"

I tossed my empty glass on the closest flat surface I could find and rested my hands on her hips even though they itched to crawl down to the curve of her ass. "Because I came out looking for a woman to please tonight. You her?"

Heat flared in her eyes, and I licked my lips when she nodded. "I am. Fuck yes, I am." Then her mouth was on mine, and I held her close and savored the taste of those plump lips, the feel of her ass in my hands.

Shit, this was a hell of a turn around, and I was excited as fuck, but I was also a skeptic. Though it felt good right now, it felt easy. *Too* easy. I pulled back and stared at her, trying to see if she had an angle or if she was the elusive mermaid, out looking for nothing but a good time. "You sure?"

She nodded and grabbed my hand. "Let's get the fuck outta here."

I wanted to question it but the sight of her ass and her legs in that itty bitty blue jean skirt made me want to find out what was underneath, and right now? My cock was in charge.

Chapter Four

Ella Mae

Okay so maybe I was a little drunker than I should have been, considering I was out on the town without any of my MC. Without any protection other than the blade inside my boot and the nine mil in my jacket. But holy shit, this dude was hot as fuck, and he knew exactly what to say to get me hot and wet and excited.

It hadn't happened in so long that it was cause enough to celebrate, but this tall drink of hot Jason Momoa-ness, hell he was like popping my cherry with a porn star. Long hair, muscles, a beard, tattoo and a smile that made my nipples hard, he was exactly what I needed to unclog the dam.

"Try to keep up cowboy."

Yep, I was just drunk enough to know this wasn't the smartest move, but sober enough to know that if I didn't listen to my body right here, right now, there was a good chance I'd die of chastity.

A low growl sounded behind me, and before I could turn around to see what kind of monster I was about to seduce, my feet were airborne and his big body pressed against the back of mine as he carried me down a dark hall to the bathrooms. I might be tipsy, but there was no fucking way in hell I'd be fucking in the bathroom at Rusty Hinges.

Thankfully, the sexy bearded biker set me on my feet and pressed my body between his and the emergency exit before he went about setting my flesh on fire with a series of kisses from one shoulder to the next, producing shiver after shiver. His deep chuckle was like a chain attached to my tits and my pussy, tugging every string until I was so turned on, I vibrated.

"I'll keep up, I just hope you can." To punctuate his point, the biker's big hand slid down the front of my body until it hit my thigh and reversed course under my skirt. He slid my panties to the side and rubbed one thick finger along the seam of my pussy. "Already soaking wet."

Fuck me, I loved a dirty talker and this dude was good. "What are you gonna do about...it." The last word came out on a moan as one thick finger invaded my poorly neglected pussy. "Thick fingers."

"Thicker cock," he assured me and nipped my ear. "Fuck, you're so wet. Did I get your sweet cunt this wet?"

Before I could answer, he was working me over, one long thick finger sliding in and out of my pussy until it pulsed and clenched around him as I felt myself barreling toward my first orgasm. I grabbed his wrist and began to grin against him.

"Yes," I bit out when he added another finger.

"Yeah, that's what you need. A big fat cock to satisfy this tight little cunt, and fuck is she tight." His thumb hit my clit and rubbed the world's fastest circles that sent me off like a batch of defective Fourth of July fireworks.

"Let go, babe. I can feel your pussy juices drip down my hand."

I arched into him, feeling the length of his cock through his jeans and when he pushed against me, a loud buzzing sounded that kind of killed the moment.

"Fuck," he growled, two fingers still buried deep in my pussy as he wrapped the other arm around my waist and carried me outside, kicking the door shut and killing that God-awful noise.

"That's better. Now where were we," he asked in a deep voice that reminded me that his fingers were still deep inside of me. "Oh yeah, right...here." He pinched my clit and I jerked my way through a powerful aftershock.

"You're beautiful when you come," he said, laughing.

"Thanks," I said, resisting the urge to roll my eyes because he seemed genuine. And the orgasm. My hands went to his waistband, but he stilled them.

"I got it."

Even better. I shrugged and leaned against the brick wall, not giving one fuck that we were about to get it on in an alley behind a roadside bar in the Texas sticks. He was hot and I was so turned on I could feel it dripping down my thighs. And that gave me an idea.

"Get it then," I told him and slid one hand between my thighs, feeling how wet and sticky I was with a groan.

"Cock hungry?"

I nodded and watched, touching myself while he unfasted his belt, his button and finally the zipper of his jeans before he shoved them down his thighs.

"Cock starved," I moaned when I saw he had a lot of cock to give me.

"Then let me fill you up." He walked to me, and as soon as he was close enough, I wrapped a hand around him, coating his long hard cock in my juices. "Oh fuck," he wailed to the stars.

"No point lettin' it go to waste, right?"

"Exactly," he growled and picked me up by the waist like I wasn't five-foot-eight and sturdy. It was nice as hell and maybe my pussy got a little wetter. Maybe.

"Oh fuck," he groaned as he impaled me on his cock, my tight cunt screaming at the sensation of being filled so completely, if too goddamn slowly.

"Don't tease," I growled, and he laughed.

"You're tight as fuck, babe. Don't want to hurt ya."

Yeah, yeah, he was a nice fucking guy. "I'll tell you when I can't take it, cowboy."

Thankfully, he took me at my word and used his chest for leverage, pressing me against the wall so he could pump his cock into me at a better, faster, deeper angle.

"Fuck," he growled when my body was finally used to how long and how thick he was, because that was when it got good. Really fucking good.

He filled me up deliciously, fucking me hard and fast, pounding into me like he hadn't been inside a pussy in a decade.

"Harder," I demanded and grabbed a handful of his hair.

The biker growled and bit down on my nipple, using the fabric of my shirt to create even more friction. He pulled hard, letting his teeth sink into the delicate flesh until my eyes began to water and only then did he release me.

"Fucking clothes," he mumbled to himself and yanked the shirt until the straps gave, and I stuck out my chest and bared my tits to him.

"Gorgeous," he growled and tasted my nipples like they were some exotic delicacy, licking and sucking and biting while his long cock pounded into me over and over. Faster and deeper he moved, like a man on a mission.

The mission was working. I felt a rush of fire through my veins before the second orgasm hit, surprising even me since I rarely came more than once in a night.

"Oh shit!" I cried as my body shook and vibrated, the surprise of it leaving me vulnerable. At the man's mercy. "Fuck!"

He flashed a brilliant grin at me and lowered me until my feet hit the pavement. "As great as those tits are, I need to get my hands on this ass." He turned me around and lifted my skirt, smacking my bare ass cheeks three or four times each.

WILD

"Yes," I moaned and pressed my face against the cool brick. It was probably dirty as fuck but between the alcohol and this man's cock, I didn't care about anything but my next fucking orgasm.

"You like that? Good because this ass has a perfect jiggle." The words were barely understandable as he gave a final smack before spreading one cheek and sliding in from the back. "Oh fuck me. What a tight wet pussy you have, my pretty."

That teased a laugh out of me, and when I tossed my head back, he took advantage, grabbing my tits with both hands and taking my mouth with his as he plowed into my pussy from the back. He fucked me hard and fast, growling into my mouth like he just couldn't get enough.

Hell, I couldn't get enough, and I was glad I didn't know this guy's name. This wasn't a random hard fuck; this was the kind of sex that left a girl dickmatized and chasing after the wrong man. But, oh, fuck, the things I could see myself doing for another ride on this cock were…*terrifying*.

"Yes! More!"

"More? You want more?"

I nodded and he let out a dark, sexy laugh.

"What do you want, this?" He wrapped my hair around his fist and tugged until my head rested on his shoulder and he could kiss me how he wanted, teasing and with lots of tongue.

"Fuck, the way you clench around me. I love a greedy little cunt," he said on a laugh and slid in and out of me, achingly slow.

At his words my pussy clenched again, flooded between us. "Happy?"

"Fucking thrilled."

Me too. I closed my eyes and savored the way he filled me up, knowing that no matter how hard it was, I had to walk away from this dick. It was too dangerous and for a woman in my position, that was a risk I couldn't take. So I enjoyed the moment for what it was, really fucking hot. He smacked my ass again and again, my pussy drenched.

"Dirty girl," he growled and nipped my ear, laughing when I pushed back against him. "Feisty too." He pulled my hair again and wrapped his other hand around my throat.

"Say when," he whispered and held me just tight enough to be scary and hot as his thick cock pumped into me.

I closed my eyes and let the sensation of falling take over as breathing became harder. I wasn't sure if it was another orgasm or the limited air and the worst part was, I didn't care. All I cared about was the pleasure that was just out of reach as his thrusts became more frantic. Fevered. "Yes!" I screamed into the night air.

With a growl, he slid deeper and deeper, holding me close and tight as pleasure worked its way to the surface.

"That's not when," he said with a playful lilt in his voice that was overshadowed by the frenzied way his hips began to move.

It was a challenge, and he wouldn't give in until I said those words, or more accurately he would force them out of me. I couldn't move and I couldn't hold onto anything, just take all the pleasure he heaped on me, more than I could stand until the word was yanked from my lips on a violent, convulsing orgasm. "When!"

His hips jerked, and I felt his pleasure hit my insides at the same moment his hand tightened around my throat until the very second things went black. When he released me, the lingering orgasm hit me more powerful than ever as he rode out his own pleasure.

"Oh, fuck woman!"

I smiled at those words. Men were brutally honest in the moments right after sex and this time, I appreciated his sentiment.

"Mission accomplished, cowboy?"

He laughed, and it took a moment for him to stand and disengage our slick, sweaty bodies even though the night air had chilled since I went inside the bar earlier.

"Mission?" he said, obviously confused.

"You found a woman and you pleased her. You pleased the fuck outta her. Seriously."

That smile was deadly. It was sweet and charming, and I was half-tempted to give him my panties just because.

"Glad to hear it."

I stepped in close and wrapped my arms around this big sexy beast of a man, pressing my lips to his because I needed another taste of the man who reminded me what I was missing out on. His hands went straight to my ass, squeezing the cheeks and letting the tip of one finger graze my opening.

"Thanks."

"My pleasure. Truly."

His smile was the last thing I saw before I turned and made my way back to my bike on shaky legs. I needed a minute, maybe five, but eventually my head was clear enough and my legs were steady enough to get me home.

Where I dreamed about the long-haired biker all night, reliving every moment with my clit-sucking G-spot vibrator.

Chapter Five

Slayer

Holy. Fucking. Shit. Did that really just happen? The cool air against my cock said yes, the hottest chick on two legs had just given me a dirty orgasm behind the goddamn Rusty Hinges. She was one hot and feisty bitch, and best of all, she knew what she wanted and wasn't afraid to go after it.

I really appreciated that in a woman.

I appreciated it even more that she liked to fuck the same way I did, hard and fast with reckless abandon that left me with my dick out in a back alley. That thought put the smile right back on my face as I tucked my still wet cock back in my pants and fastened them before anyone else came out here and got the wrong idea.

Footsteps sounded behind me just as I got my zipper up but I turned too late to identify the fucking dead man who'd just sucker punched me.

"What the fuck?"

The asshole got me right in the nose, but luckily my shit was too tough to break. I got on my feet and took a fighting stance until my vision un-blurred.

"Stay away from her!"

Her? Who the fuck is her? Before I could ask the question, the douche hit me again, square on the jaw, and my legs wobbled, not because his hit had any real power, but because that fucking orgasm had left them weak.

"What," I muttered as I pushed that fucker against the wall because I refused to go down. "The fuck?"

"I said stay the fuck away from her!" The dude was fucking insane, he had that crazed crackhead look in his eyes, and he practically vibrated with nervous energy. Couldn't weigh more than a buck fifty. Had to be high on something.

"Who the fuck is *her*? And if you don't answer me, the next time you hit me, I'm fucking you up."

The dude snorted but my words gave him pause. I let him go with a shove. He ranked a hand through thick curls and blew out a breath.

"Chance. Stay the fuck away from Chance or you'll regret it, motherfucker!" He gave me one last, disgusted, look and walked away.

I shrugged and rubbed my jaw. It wasn't the first time a pissed off ex, or current lover, got mad that I had a taste of what he mistakenly thought was his. Didn't matter, unless that piece of shit thought he could sucker punch me again, chances were good I'd never see that stacked brunette again.

So Chance was her name? I was pretty sure it was after that shitshow, but I definitely wouldn't be seeing her again if these were the types of games she played. I didn't mind a good hard fuck, and if it was casual that was even better, but I didn't involve myself in unnecessary drama. I couldn't afford to when the MC got in plenty of trouble without my help. And it seemed that sexy bitch was up to her pretty brown eyes in trouble.

Thanks, but no thanks.

I made my way to my bike with a smile on my face, thinking about those big teardrop tits and the way they bounced when my cock slid deep in her tight cunt, and holy fuck it was tight. That was why I wasn't worried about the limp dick blond. If he fucked her recently, he wasn't getting the job done, and if he hadn't, well he'd probably never get another sniff of those sexy panties she wore. Neither would I, but I wasn't looking for anything more than what I'd gotten tonight.

That didn't mean I wouldn't take another dip inside that sweet pussy if given a chance, but I wouldn't go out looking for it. Or for her. Chasing a woman, especially one I'd already had wasn't my jam, so I slotted her into my leggy bad girl fantasy spank bank and enjoyed the sound of my bike roaring to life.

It was a short drive back to Opey this time of night, or morning, I didn't even know what time it was, and I took my time, weaving through the streets of the idyllic-looking small town. This was exactly the kind of place I'd dreamed of living in when I was a kid, with big houses and wraparound porches, spacious backyards and grass that needed mowing each week. I dreamed of paper routes and summer jobs until I realized that would never be my reality.

Then I smiled, because somehow, after a lifetime of chaos and violence and war, I'd finally gotten the small-town life I wanted. And it was more often than not, boring as a motherfucker.

Nights like tonight didn't come around often, and hell, I'd be a true asshole to wish for more MC drama considering how many people had died or were injured, myself included. It was all in the name of protecting the Reckless Bastards and the people who mattered to them, so it was a small price to pay to live in a world where I could thrive.

My turn signal indicated a left but about two blocks back I noticed that I'd picked up a tail somewhere in town. A dark-colored sedan that looked to be from the nineties, maybe early two thousands, followed me about a block back. Lights off, which only made him more suspicious. I went right and sure as shit, the dark sedan followed. I didn't want to wake up all of Opey since it had to be past midnight. Most of the town was already tucked in bed, so I took the main road that led to the ranch, meandering around the various dirt and service roads until I could get behind him.

Just before I reached the strip of land that ended the Opey town limit and started Oakley, I found my spot. A dark blue Chevy Lumina, definitely late nineties model and not from Texas. I pulled up beside him since ours were the only two vehicles on the road and motioned for him to roll down the window.

He did, the idiot.

"Do we have a fuckin' problem?" I didn't recognize the dude as belonging to any organization we did business with, or any who might have a beef with the Reckless Bastards. Hell, I didn't recognize him at all. He had dark brown hair and hazel eyes, no noticeable tattoos. Or patches.

But the fucker *did* have a staring problem, boring a hole into me instead of answering my damn question.

"I don't know you," he said over the noise of my bike.

"Pull over, we'll get to know each other *real* well," I told him with a wide smile.

"No need. You're not who I was looking for." But the quick look down at my vest said he knew who I was or at least who the Reckless Bastards were, and that meant he was looking for a brother.

"Who *are* you looking for?"

"Not you," he growled and sped up.

"I don't think so motherfucker!" I flipped my windscreen down and hit the gas, following the fucker until I caught up with him and cut him off, almost. He was good behind the wheel, too good, and managed to avoid spinning out but not passing me.

He straightened the car and hit the gas, but my bike was easier to maneuver than his twenty-year-old car. I managed to stay ahead of him, just enough to piss him off. Good. I was suddenly in the mood to cause some trouble, and this fucker was looking for trouble.

It was a perfect match.

The idiot laid on his horn, and I risked a look back to see that he had slowed down. I did the same, keeping a healthy distance between us.

Finally, we came to a turnout and he pulled off the round, I slowed down and pulled my bike close to his car. I got off my bike, hit the kickstand and waited to see his next move.

He got out of his car and leaned on one of the big ass fenders. I shrugged, waiting for him to say, or do, something.

"Well?" I said to break the tension.

"I said I ain't lookin' for you," and I detected a hint of an accent, but I couldn't figure out from where.

"Tell me who you're lookin' for and we can end this."

"Can't do that. It's personal."

That shit didn't make sense. "The *who* is personal, too?"

He nodded and folded his arms, leaning against the front of the car with his long legs crossed at the ankles. "Yep."

"Then we got a problem. Give me a name and we'll go our separate ways."

The man pulled a gun, long and nickel plated, and waved it like that shit was supposed to scare me. "Or I can just go about my business the way I planned."

It was funny because he thought it would work. It wouldn't. I showed off a gun of my own, two of them in fact, and aimed one at him. "You could."

He calculated his odds and figured out the same math I already had. His six shooter didn't have shit on me and given his age, at least twenty years older than me, my aim was probably a hell of a lot more accurate. "I ain't lookin' for trouble."

"I believe ya, just tell me what you are lookin' for?"

His shoulders fell. "My kid."

That was exactly the kind of personal shit I wanted no part of. I made sure I didn't create any babies I couldn't account for, which only made me think of taking that brunette raw behind the alley. A fuckup on my part. "If you're looking for a kid, why are you out following me this time of night?"

"Thought you might lead me to her."

"No fucking shit." The question was why he thought that and all the reasons that came to mind were un-fucking-palatable. "Got anything else to say?"

The dude shook his head, and we stood there, staring at each other, both of us trying to figure out what the fuck to do next. "Nope."

"Then the way out of town his that way. I suggest you take it and don't look back."

"And if I don't?"

"I'd be surprised if you live long enough to regret it." I was done talking to this asshole. I'd kick his ass happily right now, but he refused to talk, which meant he had to get the fuck outta town.

With nothing but a nod he got in his car, and started the engine. I followed him as he drove past the Thanks for visiting Opey sign. He kept driving at the Welcome to Oakley sign, and I watched until his taillights disappeared.

Two chance encounters.

What a weird fucking night.

Chapter Six

Ella Mae

The sting of the hot water on my flesh was nice and relaxing, not to mention how well it soothed my aching muscles. That long-haired hottie with the beard was exactly what my mind and my body needed tonight. I hadn't been fucked in a long time, and I couldn't remember the last time I'd been fucked that good, which meant I should be operating at maximum capacity for the next few weeks.

That was exactly what I needed to get back on track. Hell what the Lords needed because shit kept coming at us. If it wasn't one thing it was another, and as second in command I needed to make sure my head was screwed on straight to make sure we met each obstacle with brute force and came out on top. It was the only acceptable option. The only way forward.

I stepped from the shower, enjoying the hot steam swirling around me and the way it made everything a little hazy. Hazy was how I felt now, post-orgasm, like everything was the same as before but now it had a little extra glow. An extra haze. I slipped on a robe and stepped out of the bathroom inside my small two-bedroom bungalow. I needed my own space just like the other Lords, and this place was all mine. Decorated in black, white and yellow, it was my personal space and no one got in without an invite.

Almost no one. I was in the kitchen grabbing a beer to help me unwind before bed when I heard a noise in the living room. On instinct, I reached for a knife and thought better of it, reaching instead for the backup piece I kept stored under a small sauce pan. With slow, steady steps I made my way toward the living room, my piece leading the way.

I recognized the familiar head of blond hair immediately, but still, I didn't lower my gun. "What the fuck, Leon?"

His gaze landed on mine and slid lower, taking in what he could see of my cleavage and legs in the floor length robe. It was impossible to miss the heat and the hunger in his green eyes, but it no longer did anything for me. Well that wasn't true, it had the power to piss me off.

"You look good, Ella. Really good." He licked his lips and reached for his cock, tugging on it like that shit was somehow sexy.

"I know. What the fuck are you doing in my house Leon?"

He smiled and stood. "This used to be our house."

"No. You used to stay here, but this place was never yours and it still isn't." I held a hand out for the key I'd only suspected he had until this moment.

"Come on, Ella. What more do you want from me?"

"Shit, that's what I want Leon. I don't want one fucking thing from you other than for you to leave me alone." And since that didn't look like it was gonna happen any time soon, I was at a loss.

"I can't do that. I love you. We belong together." Yeah, he was becoming certifiable with those wide, glassy eyes and newfound perma-twitch.

"No, we don't."

"Yeah? Then why'd I fuck up that asshole tonight?" He growled in anger.

I frowned and crossed my arms. "What asshole?" If he caused shit at the Rusty Hinges, Curt would lose his shit, and I'd be the one to take it. All of it.

"That dirty fucking biker from the bar, the one who took advantage of you!" One hand slid through his hair and scraped down his face, hard and rough. "I can't stand the thought of his fucking hands on you like that, and I took care of it. I wouldn't have done that if I didn't love you. If we weren't meant to be, baby."

Baby! I hated when he called me that shit. "He didn't do anything to me that I didn't ask for, Leon. Jesus, what the fuck is wrong with you?"

"I had to defend your honor!"

"My honor? Fuck you! I wanted it! I asked him to fuck me, begged him for it." That was the truth of it, whether or not he could handle it was another matter.

Leon shook his head, trying to block out my words by hitting the side of his head. "No! You would never cheat on me. You *love* me!"

At one time, I did. "That was a long time ago, Leon."

"You could love me again."

I shook my head, sad and angry. "I tried and tried. You made it impossible, and now I'm over you, Leon. You need to move on before things get ugly." *Uglier,* in fact since the guy who fucked me so good also happened to be a member of the Opey, TX chapter of the Reckless Bastards, an MC with ties to Las Vegas. Saw the patches on his *kutte*. If he made the connection between me and Leon and the Lords of Buckthorn, it could get ugly as shit.

"It's already ugly. You chose Curt over me," he whined.

"Bullshit. You made the wrong choice and you're pissed I didn't blow up my life with you. And once again, you've fucked shit up because you only ever think of yourself, Leon. Fuck!"

This shit with the Reckless Bastards could get ugly, which meant it was on me to fix this before Curt even got wind of it. "What happened to you?"

He snorted. "I fell for the wrong girl."

"That's your problem, Leon. You always looked at me like I was a little girl. I never was." I hadn't been a girl since I left home at fifteen, but Leon wanted to be the big man so badly, he cast me in a role that was never suitable for me. "Listen to me if for no other reason than I used to love you. Stop following me. Stop making trouble. And for fuck's sake, get the hell out of Texas."

"Can't do it, babe. Not without you."

"You can and you will." If, not *when* it came down to Leon or the Lords, there was no fucking question about where my loyalties lie. "If you break into my house again, I'll put a bullet between your eyes." I went back to the kitchen to retrieve my unopened beer and chugged the icy liquid down my throat. When I got back to the living room, Leon was still there, head in his hands, lost in thought.

"I regret bringing you on. Introducing you to the fucking Lords of Buckthorn."

I knew he did. He'd said it all the time when I started moving up the ranks as a woman in the MC. He hated it, and I believed it played a big role in the mess he was today.

"It was the best gift you ever gave me, Leon." The club shaped the woman I was today, and I could never regret that.

Ever.

"Then you owe me."

"I've paid any debt I might owe you." He had no clue how much he owed me for the fact that he was still alive and kicking after he followed me all over Texas. "More than you know."

"Bullshit. It's all about the Lords with you now."

I nodded because it was true. The leadership responsibility I had was one I took seriously. These guys were my brothers, my family and so were the Ladies of Buckthorn, including my own kid sister. I'd lay down my life for them. "Then you should know what I'll choose if you keep pushing the issue."

He stood with a creepy smile. "You can't kill me, Ella Mae. I'm your first love."

He wasn't. He was my second love, actually.

"I can kill anyone I need to, Leon. Remember that." He did hold a special place in my heart, but not the place that would ever put him above the MC. Leon was a liability and the more I looked at him, smiling wildly without any fucking clue that I was the reason he was still breathing, the more I wondered what the hell I ever saw in him.

"Then why am I still alive?"

I snorted in disgust and took a step back. "Because apparently I'm the type of chick who needs to learn a hard lesson twice." A mistake I wouldn't make again.

Chapter Seven

Slayer

"Waking up with an empty sac should feel a fuck of a lot better than this." After gettin' it on with that hot chick in the alley behind Rusty Hinges and then catching an unexpected ass whooping from that insane asshole, you'd think the tight cunt would have stuck with me more. Instead it was my black eye.

"At least he didn't break your nose." Gunnar, the fucker, could barely suppress his laughter.

Yeah, at least. "You ever heard of anyone named Chance?" That shit had bugged me until I drifted off to sleep. Who the fuck was Chance? The obvious answer was that leggy brunette, but I needed to know.

"Nope. But there ain't any chicks I'd have reason to do business with outside of The Barn Door," he said with a shrug, his gaze focused on the horizon. "It was probably his old lady, or more likely an *ex*-old lady."

"That's what I figured, too." Still, something about that dude didn't sit right with me. Apart from the fact he busted up my face.

Gunnar smacked my arm to get my attention. "What's eating at you? Did you catch feelings for that chick or something?"

My brows dipped and furrowed. "Fuck no, but if I find out who *Chance* is, then I can find *that* fucker and beat his fucking ass." And that would be a fucking delight, for him to see the beatdown coming. "Plus it's a little weird he was there, right?"

"Yeah." Gunnar pushed off the post and clapped me on the back. "Sounds like you've stumbled into some stalker type shit. Just leave it off Hardtail, would ya?" His lips may have smiled, but I didn't miss the steeliness behind his blue gaze.

"Don't plan to do anything other than return an ass kickin'."

"Good to hear. Let's go back in and this time, try not to make my son cry."

I barked out a laugh. "It was a shock to him to see my pretty face so bruised up. He'll get used to it." He'd have to considering how things had shaken out with the MC the past few years. "Stone, my man! Sup?" I held out my fist against his tiny one, and he looked up at me and grinned.

Then burst into tears. "Do something about that, would ya?" Peaches motioned to my face with a frown. "He's barely settled down from ten minutes ago."

Whatever. "Fine, coffee and then I'm out." I went to the pot that had just finished brewing and poured one of the colorful oversized mugs Peaches had restocked the kitchen with recently. When it was teetering on dangerously overflowing, I stopped and turned to the table with a half-smile. "See you guys later."

"Bye Uncle Slayer!" Maisie, Gunnar's preteen little sister, held a wide smile but I could tell even she was a bit terrified of my face.

"Keep an eye on them, would you, Maze?"

"I will," she said eagerly, all traces of fear gone at the thought of being in charge.

I made my way across the property to my own little place I'd built over the past few years. I refused to call a cabin because I wasn't the type of guy to live in a cabin. And unlike the rest of the guys, I didn't build a cabin, but a small ranch-style house because it was nice to come home to at the of each day. After so many years bouncing around, first the country and then the world, it was nice to see the blue trim after work.

Inside, I set the coffee down, got undressed again and drifted off to sleep, more exhausted than I realized, because some time later a loud and obnoxious banging sound woke me up from a dirty dream.

"All right," I grumbled, figuring it was Peaches trying to scam someone into babysitting. Again. "Go away."

The knock grew louder and more insistent, and I kept right on ignoring it. Until the doorknob started to jiggle. I sat up and scanned the room to make sure I was alone. Another round of knocking started, and I got up and yanked a pair of boxers off the laundry basket before heading to the door. "What. The. Fuck?"

It was the last damn person I was expecting to see. She looked even hotter in the light of day.

"Not the good southern manners I was expecting, but I can manage. Slayer, right?"

The hot as fuck brunette from last night stood in front of me with her hands on hips I knew fit perfectly in my hands. She wore a pair of painted on black jeans and a gray t-shirt that hugged her tits perfectly.

"Hello?"

I blinked until I could see something other than those long shapely legs and huge tits. Until her face came into focus and on the heels of that, the memory to explain the frown on her face.

"Yeah, I'm Slayer. And I'm guessing you're Chance?"

She nodded and held out a hand. "Ella Mae, actually but most people know me as Chance."

I looked at her extended arm trying to figure out if she was just fucking with me, then my gaze slid back up to hers.

"Here to ease your guilty conscience? Don't bother and *don't* come around here again."

I shut the door, brave—or crazy—bitch that she was, she pushed it back.

Ella Mae, or *Chance*, wasn't put off by my tone which would have impressed me if she wasn't playing games. "I deserved that. I guess."

"You guess? What was that in the alley exactly? An attempt to make your boyfriend jealous so he'd move in or ask you to marry him, or some other stupid high school shit like that?"

I raked a hand through my hair, realizing it was tangled as fuck, and I couldn't bring myself to give a damn. Still, I stepped back so she could enter if she wanted, turning my back to her. I leaned against the half wall that separated the kitchen and the living room.

"You're pissed."

"Something like that," I admitted and crossed my arms, a move Chance tracked with a heated gaze.

She nodded and straightened her spine. "Look, I'm sorry about what happened after I left. I should have taken care of Leon a long time ago but old loyalties and all that. Anyway, I didn't realize he was following me."

"How long has he been your ex?"

"Officially a year and a half but closer to two, and he's had a hard time accepting it. We were together a long time so I was trying to give him time to get used to the idea, but last night," she trailed off, realizing she said too much.

"What?"

"Nothing."

"Ella Mae."

She arched a brow, and I folded my arms and arched a brow of my own. "He was in my place when I got out of the shower."

What the fuck? "Why are you so calm about this guy? He's clearly unhinged."

"I'm dealing with it. That's why I came here. When Leon admitted he'd *defended my honor,* I knew I had to find you."

There was more she wasn't saying, but I was more focused on something else. "How did you find me?"

"Your *kutte.* You had it on last night." She gave a shrug as if that answered the question, but I was half impressed she'd tracked me down and turned on at the way her nipples slowly hardened under my gaze.

"Well, your ex sounds like a problem, one you need to deal with right away."

"I will. Believe me." I didn't know this woman from any other, but I believed the hardness in her voice. It made me wonder about her, something that rarely happened when it came to women.

Too bad those fucking nipples were all I could think about. Mostly.

"You and what army sweetheart?"

She sent me a glare I expected and licked her lips. "Wouldn't you like to know?"

Fuck yeah, I would. "No," I told her instead, smiling as I pushed off the half wall and closed the distance between us, giving Chance plenty of time to take in the sight of me in nothing but my drawers. "There is something else I'd like to know though."

Heat fired her eyes into melted gold, and she swallowed. "Yeah? What's that?"

Her tone was husky, and that little pulse at the base of her neck beat a dance track.

"How those sweet lips of yours would feel wrapped around my cock."

I stood still, waiting for a kick to the nuts or a knife to the gut because Chance looked like the type of chick who fought back, *and* was armed.

That thought turned me on for some fucked up reason, and when she licked her lips again and put one hand on the waistband of my boxers, I lost all ability to think.

Maybe it was just a dream. Hell, maybe her ex hit me harder than I realized.

Chapter Eight

Ella Mae

I'd be lying if I said that I hadn't thought about sucking this big hunk of a man off, but the alley wasn't the time or the place. But right now, with him standing and glaring down at me while his abs glistened and that long brown hair looked like someone had already tangled her fingers in it? Lucky bitch. His cock twitched behind red cotton, which both surprised me and turned me on since he seemed like an all-black wardrobe kind of guy to me.

I gripped the waistband with one hand, and the backs of my fingers brushed against the bristly hairs that surrounded his cock. The other hand moved like it was stuck in mud, lifting in the air and reaching into the waistband so I could feel the heat and weight of his long, thick cock. Today the lights were on and the fucking sun was shining, and I could see everything.

Every. Fucking. Thing.

The way Slayer kept his beard trimmed *just* so in that way meant to keep every pair of panties in any given room soaked. Dripping, in fact. His brown eyes were just about black with desire, his smooth skin on just the right side of sun-kissed. The left side of his body from his pec down to his wrist was covered in images that blended into one another hypnotically. Tantalizing.

And then I got to the real show, yanking down his red boxers so I could take in all of him. Every beautiful thick inch of him. I gave his cock a squeeze and he groaned.

"It ain't a stress ball sweetheart."

"I wouldn't be so sure about that," I told him with a grin and a few good tugs on that long beautiful cock. The way it throbbed in my hand and the thick vein on the underside pulsed with need had me wet, wanting him. Now. "Enough talking," I said.

His deep chuckle was the only response before one hand raked down my hair and tangled, purposely, in his fingers. He gave it a good tug until the front of my neck was exposed to him. Then his tongue started at the base of my throat at my racing pulse and scraped up to my chin. He nibbled my chin and across my jaw with a groan.

"You're a bossy little thing."

"Not bossy," I panted with a smile.

"A little bossy." He gave my hair another tug and my pussy clenched with need, dripped with desire.

"You don't like bossy women?" His hand loosened, and I dropped down in front of him, fisting his beautiful cock with both hands, being a little rough because I knew a guy like him could take it.

"Fuck," he growled and dropped his head back as his hips flexed. "Nope. No problem at all."

"Good. Now shut up." I smiled up at him and when he opened his mouth to speak, I wrapped my lips around the angry, swollen head of his cock. And sucked.

"Fuck, woman!"

I smiled but I wouldn't let any amount of praise distract me from this perfect, beautiful cock. It was long, about nine inches and just thick enough to make me ache, because holy fuck-a-moly was I aching right now. Deep down in my pulsing, clenching, wet fucking pussy, I already ached.

But I wasn't one of those women who shied away from a cock. Oh, hell no! Especially one as nice and thick as this one. I wanted him to fuck me hard. Tear me up. Let me know what kind of a man he was.

But first, I took him deep, all the way to the back of my throat. And every uttered 'fuck' and every grunt of 'holy shit' didn't just turn me on, no, it made me fucking crazy. I sucked him off the way Leon always wanted me to, but that asshole never inspired my inner slut this way.

"Oh fuck! Yes!" His hips moved, a little but his hands found their way back to my hair, wrapping the length around his fists...but that was it.

I waited for him to start fucking my throat, to ram his big cock down there but he didn't. I risked a look up and all I could see were the bunching muscles of his throat and jaws, flexing with restrained desire. *God he was fucking beautiful*. More so when he was in the throes of passion, and I wanted to see more.

"Chance, fuck!"

I smiled around his cock, sucking hard until only the tip was in my mouth. Then I was empty and moaned at the feeling, but I wasn't done with this fine man. Not yet. I jerked his cock and licked and sucked his sac, enjoying the way he tried so hard to be a gentleman.

Gentlemen were overrated.

"Slayer." His brown eyes popped open, brows furrowed in an angry expression I found endlessly hot. "Show me how you like it."

He growled and shook his head.

"Yes." I teased him, sliding my tongue back and forth against the slit at the head of his cock.

"Fuck!"

Still, his hips moved in long slow strokes. Nice. I wanted more than that, and I gripped his ass and pulled him forward, taking him as deep as I could before swallowing around the tip.

"Fuck!" Much better. His hips started to move in shorter strokes. Faster strokes. Every time he thrust, a sexy growl escaped, and I felt my body vibrate.

"Fucking, Chance," he growled and held me still while his cock stroked against my tongue. In and out. In and out.

He slid so deep I choked and when Slayer tried to step back, I squeezed that fine ass and made him stay where he was.

"Dirty fucking girl," he growled and slid his cock down my throat—deep—one last time. He stayed there for several seconds, and I felt every drop of need slide down my thigh.

"Stop!"

The loud sharp bark shocked a gasp out of me, and I felt my nipples bead. "Well? How do my lips feel on your cock?"

He smiled at me and *goddamn* it only ratcheted up my desire to about ten million. "Pure fucking bliss."

Good. "Too bad you didn't finish." I wasn't a come-guzzler but when a cock was just right, well a girl took one like a champ.

"I want to be inside that tight wet cunt of yours. Again." He shivered like even the memory of my pussy was too much and fuck me, I was hella flattered.

"Yes. That."

He was in front of me in a flash, on his knees in front of me, and I couldn't look away. His big thick fingers worked clumsily on the buttons of my jeans. They were a fucking hassle but totally worth the way he looked at my legs when the door opened. It took a minute but Slayer made quick work of my jeans and let the cute pink thong stay where it was. "Next time wear a fucking dress."

Before I could tell him he should worry about satisfying me this time, Slayer pushed me and I fell over the arm of the sofa, feet hanging in the air wildly.

"Fucker."

"Not yet. Soon." His big hands gripped my thighs and held them wide open and I knew there would be ten little circle bruises on my inner thigh, and I couldn't bring myself to give a damn. Not when he smiled down at me just as his tongue slid inside my pussy.

"Oh fuck!" He was an expert level pussy tamer, using that big fat tongue and those flexible lips to bring me to the heights of desire. Over and over again. "Fuck!" I couldn't find one spot to hold on to, to grab, so I chose my tits, giving him a little show while he drove me out of my fucking mind.

"Damn you taste like coconuts." When he said those words and followed them up with the most thorough pussy licking of my life, all I could do was accept it. Take the tongue lashing he gave me and explode in orgasm. Happily. Hungrily.

"Oh fuck, shit yeah!"

Slayer laughed but that was his only sign of stopping, his tongue kept moving slowly over my swollen clit. "Tongue tied?"

"You...wish," I moaned when one thick finger slid inside my pussy. And then two. "Fuck me."

"Soon," he growled and pumped his finger in and out of my pussy, hard and fast while his tongue moved slowly and teased my clit until a second, more powerful orgasm washed over me.

"Enough," I panted even as need still pulsed through me.

"Enough?"

I shook my head with a smile. "Not even fucking close. Show me whatchoo got, Slayer."

"My absolute fucking pleasure."

That damn smile was a killer, but when his cock slid into me this time, I wasn't thinking about anything but how long I would last before another orgasm rushed over me.

"Think. That's. My. Line."

Another one of those growl-y laughs erupted from him but it didn't stop his flow, oh no, his hips moved like the man danced for a living, loose and flexible as they pumped into me, his big cock filling me to the point of aching. "So fucking…tight."

"More."

He moved so quick, growling as his cock slid from my body, leaving me cold and lonely while he marched around the sofa and sat down. "You want more? Come fuckin' get it."

Hell yes, please. I wiggled, inelegantly, off the sofa and stood in front of him, taking off the rest of my clothes before sliding onto his lap. From this angle his cock felt massive. Thick and invading but I was so wet, so loose and so ready it was the most delicious friction.

"Yes!" I said wildly as I tossed my head back and gripped the back of the sofa, riding him hard and fast, like a woman possessed. His cock was delicious and even though my thigh muscles screamed, I kept going. And going.

And going.

We were slick with sweat and panting so hard our breaths came out like truck engines, and we smiled goofily as we both pumped and ground against each other, chasing after pleasure. Slayer's hand went to my ass cheeks and spread them wide. "More," I growled in his ear and nipped it hard.

He held two fingers up to my mouth. "Lick."

I opened my mouth and thoroughly sucked his index and middle finger. "Done."

That hand slid down my waist and to my hips before sliding back around to my ass. Then, my asshole. Slowly the finger entered my ass and instead of slowing down, I rode his cock harder. Faster. That finger went deeper and deeper, until I was filled up.

No, not everywhere. My mouth, hungry and empty, found his. We kissed and we fucked while he filled me up everywhere. It was hard and fast, it was rough. Blessedly rough. "Slayer!"

"Chance!"

Faster and faster, I rode his cock and his finger, looking right at him as pleasure worked its way through my body. "Yes, Slayer. More."

It was like one of those flashover fires where one minute everything was quiet and still, almost lifeless while we stared at one another, lost in the moment. Then the next second it was explosive. Combustible. Nuclear.

My body shook and twitched, and Slayer gripped me so tight I knew I would be bruised everywhere. He shouted and growled my name, body jerking as he found his own never-ending release.

"Holy fucking shit woman."

I flashed a panting smile up at him, my pussy still pulsing and leaking around him. "I gotta admit, you taste better than I expected."

He growled and stood with me in his arms, heading down a long hall that ended in an overly-masculine bedroom complete with a California king size bed. "This time, I'm gonna take my fucking time."

And he did. He really fucking did.

Chapter Nine

Slayer

Goddamn fucking goats. Yep, this was my life now. In between kicking the shit out of whatever idiots were dumb enough to cross the Reckless Bastards, I tended to goats. Fucking goats.

It's not like I was being singled out, not really unless I *was*. Everyone did their rotations listening to Holden talk about the beauty and fertility of the land and all that other livin' off the land bullshit. The problem was, it was my turn to tend to the fuckers and they were, hell they were wily as shit. "Get your ass back here right now, Grendel!"

That damn goat was the oldest of the bunch, and the one most likely to wander off. I managed to catch up with the old fucker and return him to the barn just in time to catch one of the newest kids, Mayhap, before she got out.

"Damn wanderers." It was the only thing about them that made them tolerable.

And kind of fucking cute.

Still, I grumbled and left the goats behind in the stable when I got busy repairing their pen. Again. It was the second time this week they managed to get out and make a run for it but when I said that to Hazel, I was the asshole with the problem. So I kept my grumblings to myself as I got rid of the chicken wire and used wood and a heavy, metal latch. If these fuckers got out of this, then they had my permission to run.

Even though I hated ranch work, it was easy. Physical labor I could do with my eyes shut. It was how I paid my way until I joined up at eighteen, and it was what I did before I found Gunnar and Hardtail Ranch. Didn't mean I liked the shit, though, especially out in the sun and with animals. Still it was easy, and today I was grateful for the mindless work because it gave me time to do something I didn't do a whole hell of a lot. Think.

I *think*. I wasn't a fucking idiot, but I also wasn't much for introspection, looking inside and overanalyzing shit in search of a deeper meaning. That was not my thing. I took people at face value as much as I could, and I expected people to tell the truth, period. End of story.

But today I couldn't stop my thoughts from wandering to Chance. Ella Mae. That name didn't suit her, it was too sweet, too innocent, and vulnerable, which weren't words I'd associate with the fiery brunette. She was strong and independent, giving off a heavy bad ass vibe, but despite all that, she was a chick who let her ex run around un-checked. She was either stupid or there was more to the story than she let on.

Either way it was a big fucking problem for me because I was eager as fuck to get my hands and my mouth on Chance again. It really was too bad that everything about her screamed trouble. An unruly ex who followed her around, an *I don't give a fuck* attitude combined with that sinful body that would bring men to blows over her. It was the kind of trouble I didn't have room for in my life.

Which was too bad, because Chance was hot as fuck and she wasn't shy, two things I appreciated in a good lay. Every fucking time I closed my eyes all I could see was her down on her knees, sucking me off like it was the only thing in the world she wanted to do. Gold-flecked eyes smirked and teased me while she took me deep and practically begged me to fuck that pretty little mouth. "Shit!"

"You all right, man?"

I turned with wide eyes to Ford and his fucking baby face. "I'm good man. I didn't hear you come up. Working on your ninja skills?"

He shrugged and raked a hand through his thick blond hair. The kid was built like a brick shit house with the face of a twelve-year-old choir boy, and the ladies couldn't get enough of him. As soon as this fucker was patched, he'd be fighting pussy off with a stick.

"They could come in handy around here. Need some help?"

I arched my brows at him. "Gunnar send you to check on me?"

He nodded. "Yeah, he asked me to see if the goats were giving you shit again." Even the prospect couldn't contain his smile over the breakout kings of Hardtail Ranch.

I snorted. "Seems me it should be Hazel or at the very least, Saint taking care of these fuckers." He couldn't say no to her but neither of them did a damn thing for these goats.

"Probably. So…help?"

We both stood and looked around at the completed pen. "This is finished. If it doesn't hold, then I'm done with these assholes. They can run off and join the circus for all I care." Ford wisely said nothing to my rant. "If you want to help you can help me get them back into this damn pen."

How such small creatures could get away so easily and so often was a goddamn mystery to me.

"Uh, Slayer?"

"What?"

"There should be five goats. Right?"

A dark groan slipped from my mouth, and I turned in a full circle to see which way the four-legged fuckers went. "That way," I pointed with a resigned sigh. "Toward the road."

Ford barked out a laugh, and we set off to chase the two escape artists, the oldest and youngest of the bunch.

"This is crazy. This is all crazy as shit, but at least you don't have to worry about dodging bombs."

"Amen, brother." It wasn't such a high bar, but for guys like us, it meant a hell of a lot. That was why I kept my bitching to a minimum. Goats and cows and horses weren't really my thing. I was a city boy through and through, but it was a lot better than grunt work in a fucking war zone.

"Who the fuck is that?" That thread of steel that shot through Ford's voice had me on edge and alert. Immediately. "Ten o'clock."

My gaze scanned starting at two and moving left until I saw the figure in the distance.

"Male at least six feet," I said and rattled off some of his features automatically. Ford nodded beside me. A minute later, only the highway separated us and the fucker was lucky.

"Back for more trouble man?" It was the same dark-haired man in the Chevy Lumina.

He held his hands up in a defensive gesture. "I'm not here to cause trouble."

"Yeah? That's real funny because trouble is exactly what you get when you start skulking around people's *private* property. This is Texas. We shoot first and ask questions later."

The man looked both ways before crossing the road, with the escaped goat at his side and his hands raised and visible.

"I'm just trying to make sure I have the right address. This is Hardtail Ranch isn't it?"

Arms folded over my chest, I stared at the would-be troublemaker and took a step forward. "Feels like we've been through this before, don't it?"

Ford stepped between us, a big beefy hand on my chest. "Do you have business on Hardtail Ranch?" He

WILD

was shorter than my own six-five by at least four inches, but Ford was still strong as an ox and intimidating as shit.

"I do but it's, uhm, of a personal nature." One hand slid over his brown hair, slightly shaky, but it seemed more like nerves than drugs, and I gave him a closer inspection. He didn't look familiar, but without the cover of darkness, he didn't look so menacing either.

"Look man, this is private property, and there are people here we'll protect by any means necessary, you feel me?" He nodded. "Good. Now state your business, and we'll see if we can help you out."

The man weighed his options for a moment before realizing he only had one: talk or get the fuck gone.

"All right. The name's Rocco, and I'm pretty sure the man who owns this place is taking care of a daughter I didn't know I had."

Holy shit. Ford and I stared at each other wearing matching expressions of shock at his bombshell. I recovered first. "You have a name for this man or the daughter?"

"Gunnar Nilsson. I knew his mom."

I snorted because Gunnar had already shared all about his mom and his childhood—and why he took care of his sister. "Right. You stayin' around here?"

He nodded. "The roadside motel just off the interstate into Oakley. This is my phone number." The man took a step forward and handed a strip of paper to Ford, the friendlier of us two. "I'll stick around another day or two. Maybe more."

I gave a nod, recognizing a deep need in his eyes. I didn't know yet if this dude would cause trouble for the MC, but I recognized the look. A family connection. "If there's anything to know, someone will call."

He nodded and crossed the road, walking a good hundred yards or more down to the shitty Lumina. He got in and drove off, and Ford whistled behind him.

"Gunnar's gonna be pissed to hear this." He smiled and clapped me on the back. "Times like this it's good to be just a prospect."

I laughed. "Enjoy it while you can, fucker. Your time is coming." The kid didn't know it yet, but his time was finally coming, sooner rather than later.

Chapter Ten

Ella Mae

"Next week we'll be back where we belong."

Curt flashed a satisfied smile as he looked around the room at the decision makers for the Lords of Buckthorn. We all wore matching smiles as we pounded on the table. Damn, we couldn't wait to go home.

"The big man is finally going back home," Curt yelled to a big cheer.

"Where he belongs," I called out excitedly, sending the boys into another fit of fist-pounding and whistling. It also meant The Lair was ready for us again.

"This means we gotta have a party to re-christen the club house, right?" Brick said. The Sergeant at Arms and the baddest motherfucker of all had a wide smile for each of us. "Right?"

Curt smiled. "Fuck yeah, we do. Next Thursday after church. Tell the Ladies," he said, letting the smile shine until it died on its own. "Any new business we need to discuss?"

The table fell silent as everyone waited to see who would set the tone for this part of the meeting. It was no surprise that all eyes were on me. I usually went first if I had any news business, then we went around the table in order of rank. So I took my time, not because I was afraid of Curt or any of the other guys for that matter. They were badasses in their own right, but to me they were just my boys. My brothers. But Curt was gonna lose his shit with my news, and he was already *thisclose* to dealing with Leon himself.

I said, "I do, actually."

After another long pause, Curt sighed. "Spit it out, Chance."

I didn't take offense to his words. The man would probably be early to his own fucking funeral because he was so impatient.

I sucked in a breath and said, "Leon is a bigger problem than I thought." I looked at the members gathered around and confessed that my ex had been following me, and I hadn't had a fucking clue.

"Are you sure it's him?" Brick asked, dark brows dipped into a protective frown. "It could be the Irish, the Russians or even the fucking cartels."

"I'm sure."

WILD

"How can you be so sure? He used to be one of us."

Leon and Brick had joined the Lords together, had been probies together and earned their bones together. This was even harder for him than it was for me.

"Because…" I sighed and looked Curt right in the eye as I spoke. "I fucked this guy I met at a bar. In the alley. When I left, Leon showed up and sucker punched him." The room fell silent, like my story had stolen all the oxygen from the room.

"And then when I tracked said guy down at his house…"

"Hold up," Curt said. "You fucked a dude *and* saw him again?" His lips twitched. "Does this mean you're back for good?"

I rolled my eyes. "Y'all are too damn obsessed with my sex life. I fuck, lots, I just don't tell you about it."

Brick leaned forward, intelligent green eyes picking up my thoughts before they turned to words. "Then why are you telling us now?"

"Because Leon assaulted him."

"And you like him? And you want Leon to stay the fuck away from him?" That came from Rosy, our

Treasurer, so named because of the thick crop of red hair he proudly wore.

I let out a long breath. This wasn't going to be good news for us. "Because he's a member of the Reckless Bastards." As I suspected that bit of news got everyone talking all at once and on top of each other, to the point it where it became just noise.

"Fuck, Chance!" Curt's roar cut through the noise until it was silent again. "I told you to deal with Leon, and now he's a bigger fucking liability. And you're fucking some new guy from a different club? If you don't take care of this shit permanently, I will."

I nodded, understanding the threat that was clear in his words and his tone. "I will. I promise."

"See that you do. Goddammit!" His fist hit the table. "Don't make me regret trusting you with this bullshit."

Fuck, he had to go there didn't he? "Got it." There was nothing else to say to that. Eventually everybody else moved on with new business, and I got lost in my thoughts. I took responsibility for Leon because I wanted him gone, not dead, which is exactly what he'd get if Curt had his way. But I'd have to pull up my big girl panties and take care of it.

"After all this bullshit you brought to the table, you could at least pretend you're paying attention." Curt's angry voice sliced through my thoughts, and I looked up to realize everyone else was gone.

"Just thinking about how I'm gonna solve this problem." I straightened up in my seat and looked Curt straight in the eye. "I've been trying too hard to be nice, letting our history color how I handle Leon. That shit is in the past."

He gave me a nod of approval. I'd passed go. "Well, thank Christ. Glad to hear it. A Reckless Bastard, huh?" The smirk he wore was like a girlfriend getting ready to hear some juicy gossip. "How the fuck did that happen?"

I shrugged. "He was just how I like 'em, big, brash, hairy and hot as fuck."

Curt barked out a laugh. "I almost feel sorry for him with a man eater like you. Is this gonna create a problem between us and the boys in Opey?"

"No. When I went over to his place, I explained it all." And a whole lot fucking more. So much fucking. My legs were still a little wobbly. "There's no problem on that front. He doesn't know anything about our connection to the Lords. Mine or Leon's."

Curt let out a low whistle. "Don't know if I'm impressed or terrified."

He should be both, but I just smiled. "He's history so it doesn't matter. I only went out there after I found out what Leon had done."

"And *how* the fuck did you find that out?"

Shit. I should've kept my mouth shut. "The fucker broke in to my apartment."

"Chance. This time next week I want Leon gone. Timbuktu or ten feet under, I don't give a fuck. Gone. Got me?"

"Yeah, I got you." Thanks to Leon's stalker fucking tendencies, I now had to make him a priority in my life. Again. I stood up to go. "Later," I said and grabbed my gear.

"Handle it," Curt said as a final warning before the door slammed behind me.

I drove home with my thoughts bouncing between memories of Slayer's hands doing magical things to my body and planning my next move with Leon. I *would* handle it this time, and I wouldn't bring our long history into it. It didn't matter that Leon and I managed to date through one and a half tours in the desert on behalf of the U.S. Army, and it didn't matter that I used to dream of having his blond-haired babies. *That* Leon didn't exist anymore. He was buried somewhere in the desert, but it had taken me far too long to really realize that.

This Leon? All cracked out on meth or opiates or whatever the hell else he was ingesting these days.

I parked my bike and made my way up the path to my front door. My mind was a million miles away because I didn't hear any footsteps coming up behind me, just a voice.

"Where in the hell have you been baby? I've been looking all over for you?"

Speak of the red-eyed devil. I spun around on a dime. "Leon!" I snarled. Man, was I pissed. He was the last son of a bitch I wanted to see right now. "What the fuck are you doing here?"

He frowned, apparently genuinely shocked that I didn't want to see him. When was he ever going to listen to me? "I told you, babe, I been looking for you."

I kept my curled fists on my hips so I wouldn't do damage to his punk ass. "Why? I told you to stay away. Do you have a death wish?"

His lips curled into that charming grin I used to find irresistible. Now? I just wanted to break his fucking nose.

"You ain't gonna hurt me babe."

He reached out to touch my face and I smacked his hand away.

"Don't be that way Chance."

"Leon," I said, trying to keep my voice under control. "Listen to me and please, for the love of all things holy, please *hear* me. Stay away from me and stay away from the Lords. If I see you lurking around again like some fucking stalker—"

"You bitch!" Before I could prepare for it, his fist came down on my cheek. It didn't take me down, but the hit made my knees wobble.

Too bad the motherfucker didn't actually take me down, because I was a fast learner . I dropped my helmet with my left hand and reached for my butterfly knife with the other. Leon, the stupid fuck, still had a smile on his face until the metal touched his skin.

"You ever put your fucking crackhead hands on me again, Leon, I'll kill you myself."

He wasn't convinced, not yet and that was my fault. His leash was too long, and I let him roam unchecked too many times. "If you *could* kill me, babe, I'd be dead already."

Yeah, that was my fucking fault, too. He thought it was because, well, what the hell else was he supposed to think? The MC let him go because he was a liability, not because of betrayal, so death seemed extreme. Now, not so much.

"I already told you that's a mistake I won't repeat again, Leon. Get the fuck outta here."

He leaned in close as if to kiss me, as if he'd forgotten he just hit me. "Chance, please. You know you love me."

"No, I don't, Leon. I don't even hate you. I just want you gone. If you don't go willingly, Curt will step in and handle things his way."

We both knew what that meant, even though Leon was determined to pretend everything was fine. Maybe it was the drugs or maybe this was what happened to a man when he lost everything.

He got a pleading tone in his voice and said, "I love you, Chance. I'm sorry."

Jesus, Mary and Joseph. When will he learn?

His apologies were worthless. Hell, they were less than worthless. I'd accepted them thousands of times over the years, making excuses for him and allowing him to use his medical problems as excuses. It was too much for too long, and the teary apology he issued now only pissed me off.

I grabbed my helmet and slid it on before I walked away and hopped back on my bike.

"Don't walk away from me. Chance! Don't *fucking* walk away from me!"

I hit the start button and my bike roared to life. I checked over my right shoulder and left him in a cloud of dust and probably even more pissed off.

Good. Being pissed off would make all of this easier.

Chapter Eleven

Slayer

"Hey, Big Sexy. You summoned me?" The sound of Peaches' cheeky tone made me smile. I turned away from the goat pen, filled with goats *thank you very fucking much*, to greet her.

"I did. Thanks for coming and without any extra ears." I loved Maisie, the kid was as cute as kids came, and she was always happy to see her Uncle Slayer. But damn the girl had a big mouth. Never met a secret she didn't want to share.

Peaches tossed her head back and laughed. "Baby girl does have the gift of gab, doesn't she? She's growing up too fast. Scary times." The smartest thing Gunnar did was make the Sin Room as far from her as possible. Who knows what she might overhear?

"Any-hoo, what did you need? And why so secret?"

"I need you to do your computer wizard shit before I take this to Gunnar." I knew it was bad protocol to go around my Prez's back about this shit. I'd sworn Ford to secrecy, though, under threat of death, and I needed to do some digging before I shit all over the peace Gunnar had fought so hard to achieve.

She took a step back, eyes wide and growing more pissed off by the second. "I'm not keeping secrets from my man, Slayer. Don't even ask it."

Fuck. "I'm not asking you to keep a secret. Just listen, will ya? Fuuuck."

She took her sweet ass time answering, studying my face to see if I was trying to pull her into some shit that might disturb her family.

"Okay. I'm listening," she said, but her tone of voice let me know she wasn't happy about it.

"Good." I took a deep breath and told her about my run in with Rocco. Both times, going into detail about the most recent episode. "He left his number, and I checked it out. He's staying at the Desert Palm Motel in Oakley."

Peaches smirked and rolled her eyes. "What do you want me to do, see if he was being serviced by Gunnar's mother nine months before Maisie's birthday?"

"Pretty much, yeah? Can you do that?"

She rolled her eyes and snatched the sheet of paper from my hands. "Of course I *can*, the question is if I should?"

"I get that, but if this guy is just trying to get some money out of Gunnar, I can put a bullet in his head, and we can move on. If he really is who he's claiming to be, Gunnar needs all the ammo he can get. That *you* can dig up for him."

She glared and pointed at me. "Low blow using my love of Gunnar and my ego against me."

"End goal achieved," I told her with a smile. "You'll take care of this?"

"I will. Whether I'll keep it from Gunnar or not remains to be seen. I'll give you a heads up."

"Yeah, thanks. You're a real *peach*."

She glared and laughed. "I'll let you get away with that because you still look a bit monstrous with all that bruising. You should have Aspen whip up one of those disgusting salves of hers. They work."

"Hell no. The one she gave Cruz smelled like dirty socks and asshole. I'd rather let nature do her thing than walk around smelling like a fucking toilet."

"I'll be sure *not* to tell her that. Want to come have dinner with us? Stone not might not even cry at the sight of you anymore."

"Thanks but I've got plans. Sort of."

Peaches rolled her eyes. "I'll warn the townsfolk to guard their panties."

"Don't worry, I'm only interested in the girls who leave their panties at home where they belong." Her laugh blended with mine and echoed in the open field.

"I hope you're wrong about this guy."

"I am too, that's why I don't want you to tell Gunnar. Yet."

"Tell Gunnar what?"

That deep angry booming voice belonged to the man himself. Though neither of us heard him approach, we both turned around casually. He was in a bad mood and spoiling for a fight.

"Tell. Gunnar. What?"

Peaches snorted and shook her head, hands fisted on her hips as her temper flared. "That Slayer and I are madly in love and running away together. Obviously."

She was either stupid or brave, I didn't know which.

WILD

"Peaches!" Gunnar said with a bit of a scowl. Apparently, he wasn't in a joking mood.

"What? That's what you're getting at, right? Slayer and I are sneaking out to Hazel's stupid fucking goat pen to have sex twenty minutes after I polished off the world's biggest Ruben sandwich."

She looked around with a frown and then turned her gaze up at me. "Babe you forgot the blanket."

Stupid. She was definitely stupid. I turned to Gunnar. "I asked Peaches to do something personal for me and to keep it from you. Personal but not involving my cock," I clarified with a smile.

"Talk," he insisted.

Peaches groaned and rolled her eyes at Gunnar. "What do you want to do, Slayer? We can tell him now or let him think the worst of us for…how long do you think we can keep this up?"

I didn't even want to think about it. A pissed off Gunnar would make sure I worked the fucking front desk every day for the next month. Or two. "As long as it takes."

"Perfect. Then he'll have a lot to make up for." She gave her husband a devilish smile, and I was very, very happy that Peaches was on my side. "To tell or not to tell, that is the question."

"Seriously?" Gunnar glared at his wife-to-be, half angry and half filled with affection.

"Some dude came around asking questions about the ranch, and he's claiming to be Maisie's dad."

"Real smooth, dude," Peaches snort-laughed and stage whispered beside me, shaking her head in disappointment. "Folded like a cheap suit."

"Thanks for nothing, *Peach*."

"Anytime. I'll look into this and let you boys talk."

"Traitor," I called after her, but Peaches only laughed and waved.

"Don't ask my woman to keep secrets from me." Yeah, he was looking for a fight. The question was why.

"I didn't ask her to keep it a secret. I asked her to dig first so I'd have something to bring to you when I told you. All the problems aren't yours alone to solve, man, no matter how good you are at it."

"Fuck, her father? Really?"

"That what he says but I ain't sure. That's why I called Peaches."

"I appreciate that." But he still didn't like it. "You comin' up for dinner?"

"Nah, I spent an hour chillin' with Maisie, and now I'm off to hunt down some pussy." And there was a sweet little brunette from Oakley who had just what I wanted.

"Have fun. Be safe."

"Always, brother." I held a hand out and Gunnar clasped it and brought me in for a bro-hug.

Gunnar went toward the gleaming white house in the distance, and I went the other way, towards my bike. Towards Oakley.

Towards *Chance*.

Chapter Twelve

Ella Mae

Three days of bliss, that was what I'd had since my last run-in with Leon, and I enjoyed it. Mostly because I wasn't foolish enough to think that one flick of my wrist had done what months of threats hadn't. But I took enjoyment where I could and three days without Leon had me feeling good. Relaxed. Focused.

To celebrate being so relaxed and focused, I started with a long hot bath complete with fizzy bombs and bubble bath. After slathering my skin with lavender-scented body cream, I decided to have a little fun with my favorite indulgence. Lacy, silky sexy underthings were my weakness. Also, my armor.

I had a special armoire just for my lingerie, and every time I opened it was like choosing my favorite piece of candy from the candy store. I reached for a black lace corset, threaded with purple silk because it was sexy and dirty, perfect for an evening with my man Jack Daniels and the *Mindhunter* boys on Netflix. As I padded down the hall toward said bottle of Jack, I could admit the look was ruined by the fuzzy black slippers on my feet. I wasn't expecting company tonight though, so I opted for comfort.

And warmth.

With Jack in one hand and a liter of Coke in the other, I made my way to the sofa and got comfy, safe in the knowledge that all doors and windows were locked, deadbolts included. The motion light was on out front and I'd enabled the security system and checked it twice. No one could get in, and even if they did, I was heavily armed. Ready for battle. It was the only way I could get tipsy and watch the Feds chase down serial killers. In peace.

It was like some sort of universal fucking indicator that the moment I thought or spoke of peace, someone or something came along to disturb it. Ruin it. The doorbell rang. Twice.

I glanced at the menus of my two favorite delivery options and frowned because I hadn't placed my order yet, which meant I hadn't invited the guest on the other side of the door. My stomach clenched at the thought that Leon would ruin my celebration of three Leon-free fucking days. After the second knock, I went to the door, sneaking a look through the peephole and relaxed. At least I didn't have to reach for my gun.

Hopefully.

I pulled the door open with a neutral expression on my face, totally at odds with the way my heart raced and my pulse kicked into high gear.

"Slayer. What are you doing here?"

His gaze was pure black with heat as he tried to figure out what to focus on first, my tits or my legs.

"Holy fucking shit, Chance." His chest heaved, and I swear his long brown hair blew back like a breeze had come from nowhere.

It wasn't exactly 'hello, beautiful,' but my body didn't care. She was on fire, wet with desire and ready for the good shit. I already knew from personal experience that Slayer *had* the good shit.

"Good enough for me," I growled and grabbed a fistful of his black t-shirt to yank him inside, fixing my lips to his before either one of us could ruin the moment with words.

His heavy boot kicked the front door closed, lips fused to mine in a kiss hot enough to singe my skin, growling as his rough hands slid up and down my body. The friction of those callouses sent a shock of electricity right between my thighs. The kiss went on and on, a rough clashing of teeth and lips, tongues tangling inelegantly in the intensity of our coming together.

"Chance," he moaned before he pulled back. He growled and then his tongue and his teeth marked a path of heat across my collarbone and down to my cleavage.

I clung to him, unwilling to let go while his hands and his mouth set me on fire. That's exactly what I wanted to do to him, and I grabbed a handful of that permanently mussed chocolate hair and yanked him back.

"Slayer," I growled and he smiled, a dark grin that had my pussy clenching with need.

"Chance," he said with a happy note that made my heart dance.

For just a moment, though. The sound of my name falling from his lips did terribly dirty things to me. I licked a trail of heat from the base of his throat all the way up to his chin, purring as I went. "Fuck!" I hissed.

"That's the idea." His words were dark and playful, setting the right mood for the moment. The low rumbling laugh of his hit me in all the right places, sending a shiver of heat down my spine.

"This fucking outfit," he growled as he took a step back, chest heaving and nostrils flaring. The line between anger and desire was blurred and it looked good on Slayer.

"You don't like it?"

"Fuck no, I love it. It'll look even better on the floor." Then his mouth was on my neck and moving down to my shoulders, all the while his hands cupped and grabbed everywhere he could. I shut my eyes and tilted my head back, giving him easy access to the skin he was so eager to mark and singe. The short rough grunts of frustration sounded at his inability to handle the tiny hooks down my back.

"Fuck. I'll replace it." Before his words could register, the sound of fabric tearing sounded in the air.

"Hey, that's fuckin' lace," I whined.

"I'll get you another one," he growled, gaze focused on my now bare tits for half a second before his warm, wicked mouth descended. He licked a tantalizing circle of fire around the darkened raspberry tips of my nipples, a perfect circle that kept me breathless and overheated.

"Better," I panted and yanked his t-shirt over his head, happy to let my eyes feast once again on his beautiful tanned skin and colorful artwork. Then he was naked, and I was naked, and the only thing I could focus on was his body. His pleasure. My pleasure.

Fuck, just pleasure in general.

We were stuck somewhere between the front door and the living room in a long dimly lit hall that was too small for one person let alone two. Somehow we made it work, mostly because Slayer had my back to the wall, his big body pressed against mine while his mouth made sweet love to my tits like they belonged to Marie Antoinette or some shit. He made his way down my body, leaving light kisses and not so light nibbles, letting his teeth scrape down my body.

"Slayer," I groaned when his tongue dipped between my thighs, not enough to make me scream but just enough to let him know he had my full attention. "Fuck," I wailed in pleasure.

"Soon," he growled and slipped his tongue back inside, spreading my legs so far apart that *he* was the only thing keeping me upright. He tongued my slit and sucked my clit, hard and rough. No finesse this time, like he couldn't get enough.

Hell, I couldn't get enough either.

His mouth and tongue moved at a punishing pace, barely giving me time to catch my breath before an orgasm barreled down on me, with his broad shoulders holding all of my weight. "Oh fuck!"

His laughter vibrated against my pussy, which sent another dart of need sliding through my veins.

"Such a juicy pussy," he growled and smiled up at me, mouth and chin slick with my juices. He looked so fucking hot, so delicious, I couldn't help but lean in for a taste.

"Freak," he laughed and stood, turning me to face the wall. "Been dreaming about fucking you like this all day."

"Only today?" I smiled over my shoulder, eyes closed as he spread my ass cheeks apart, massaging my pussy from behind.

"Days are long," he said simply and dipped one long finger deep inside, pulling out a long low cry. Then his thick cock was stretching me deliciously until I was wrapped tight around him, pulsing and quivering as a quick layer of sweat settled on top of my skin.

"Fuck you feel so good," he grunted as he pounded his cock into me, slow at first and then harder and deeper as the friction eased his path.

"Yes, Slayer! Yes!" I smacked the hell out of the wall beside my face because it was the only thing I could while his big body dwarfed mine, his cock thrusting deep while his chest was flush against my back. I could only stand there on shaky legs and take the fucking he gave me, arching my back to give that big cock of his the best chance of pleasing me.

"Fuck!" was all I could say.

"Chance," he grunted and slid his hands slowly up my waist until they cupped my tits, then squeezed harder and harder to match his thrusts. I was lost. Thoroughly fucking lost in the pleasure coursing through my veins and the orgasm leaking from my body.

"Shit," he growled and lifted me in the air, cock still buried deep as he made his way to the living room and the plush sofa.

"Better."

Being bent over arm of my sofa while his big cock plowed into me from behind and those heavy, meaty hands smacked my ass hard enough to leave marks was my idea of heaven. "More! Gimme more, Slayer! Now!"

Harder and harder, his hands landed on my ass and with every smack my pussy soaked us, sending the friction out of this world. It was too much. It wasn't enough. It was fucking perfect, the way his cock invaded me, hard and fast, and his hands left a white-hot stinging sensation that only heightened my pleasure.

"Chance, fuck!"

My face smashed into the crushed velvet fabric of the sofa I loved. My cries muffled as Slayer fucked me hard. He fucked me until my legs went limp through orgasm number two. After that, he wrapped my hair around his fist and tugged.

Hard.

"Slayer," I growled and arched my back because I needed to feel the full length of him buried deep. "Fuck. Me."

He gave my hair another tug until he tilted my head was tilted and arched my back perfectly. His cock hit *that spot*, the one that made me stupid. The spot that was nothing more than a myth until you found the right cock and only then did it become magical. Filthy and magical. Over and over Slayer hit it until I could no longer revel in the pleasure because it swept me under, kept me there while I rode out my orgasm and Slayer sought his out.

"Chance." The word was a warning, his hips were moving like a jack hammer and sweat dripped from his body into mine as he fucked me hard and deep, taking parts of me with him with every stroke.

"Go. Let. Go." I was breathless and damn near exhausted from the orgasms but then his cock got harder. He pulled my hair back harder and stilled, the long vein in his cock started to pump as pleasure roared out of him, leaving me a hot sticky satisfied mess.

"Oh shit, Chance." Slayer's hips bucked, and he couldn't seem to stop thrusting into me, slow and jerky moves that sent aftershocks sizzling through me, skittering over my skin. "Fuck!" I wheezed.

I smiled because, fuck yeah it felt good to bring a big biker like Slayer to his knees with my cunt. His knees buckled, and we both went down and goddammit, his cock slipped free.

Slayer laughed. "Fuck woman, you took my legs from under me."

"I did, didn't I?" I turned around and sat up to straddle him, sliding my swollen went cunt up and down the length of his fading erection because I really couldn't get enough. No, this greedy bitch was hungry for more, for another orgasm from this man, and my body wouldn't stop until she got what she needed.

"You're lookin' awful smug right now." He chuckled.

"Feelin' it too," I told him honestly as a gasp escaped at the feel of his cock, growing stiffer by the second.

"Then I guess we better do something about that." His mouth kicked up into a crooked grin as his fingers found my wet center and damp curls, playing for another minute or two until another orgasm bucked me right off his big body and onto the hard fucking floor.

"Worth it," I panted with a laugh as the fourth orgasm washed over me. And knocked me out.

All the way out.

Chapter Thirteen

Slayer

I wasn't really a morning after kind of guy. I preferred to get gone well before the sun came up, more often than not I was gone within minutes after round two. Round three if the chick could hang, but most couldn't. Not with this cock.

The fact that Chance could hang was part of the reason I was still at her house when the sun came up, in her bed ,and under her deep purple comforter, her naked body pressed tight up against mine. I didn't know why else I was here, and I was too fuck-drunk to give a lot of thought.

"You can stay until your legs work again."

I arched a brow at her laughing face. "That eager to get rid of me?" Another novel moment since usually women used all their charms to get me to stay a little longer.

"No," she sighed and pushed up to face me. "But I'm letting you know that I'm not a pussy or a whiny bitch, so if you want to leave, go ahead." Her tone was matter of fact, almost angry but not quite.

It was strange, but I was too exhausted, and I felt too fucking good to move. For now. "I'm good. When I'm not, I'll let you know."

She chuckled and laid her head on my chest, one hand slowly caressing my midsection. "I'm sure you will. Tough guy."

"You're pretty tough yourself."

She looked up with one of those dark brows arched. "Because I'm a woman?"

I grabbed a handful of her tight round ass, letting my finger graze her opening until she moaned. "Because you make sure I know that you're one tough broad."

"It's not you, it's everybody." She pulled away. It was a small move that allowed her to prop her head up in one hand and look at me. "Let people know up front that I won't take any shit, and they won't get any. Most of the time."

Sounded like she grew up on the streets. I knew kids like her, had served with plenty of them, and they were all tough sons of bitches. Loyal as hell, too. "I'm only interested in giving you orgasms, Chance. Nothing more."

WILD

She let out a dark erotic groan. "A goal I approve of fully." The smile on her face was totally satisfied, half asleep but half ready to go again. "Your accent isn't Texan."

She was fishing but not in the usual way. "Nope. Only been here the last few years. Moved around a lot as a kid and even more as a Marine."

Chance nodded and looked me over again, heat burning in her eyes as her tongue slipped out and slicked across her bottom lip. Her top lip.

"How long does it take before everything about you screams soldier?"

I shrugged. "Don't know since I'm not a solider."

She rolled her eyes. "Okay, a Marine then?"

"Don't know. Haven't given it much thought." A Marine was as much of who I was as a biker, a fighter, a shit starter. A womanizer. "You pegged me as military at the Rusty Hinge?"

"Not military necessarily but some type of institutionalization. Police or military or prison would've all been a good guess. The way you carry yourself, with a kind of certainty that comes from being, I don't know, a real bad ass."

I had to chuckle at that. "You can do better than that, Ella Mae."

She glared at me, and I laughed. "Maybe I could but half the blood in my body is still in my clit. So cut me a break and tell me, do you actually do cowboy shit on that ranch of yours?"

Her question surprised the hell out of me. Most women, well most local women wanted to know more about the money the ranch made and very little else. "You asking me about my work, Chance?"

"No, I'm asking you to give me some material for my flick bank."

"Your flick bank?"

She nodded, exasperated. "Yeah, it's like a spank bank but for a woman. Now give up the goods. You wear leather chaps and no shirt because it's always so hot, and you're always so sweaty, right?"

She teased another laugh out of me, not just with her words but the way she closed her eyes as if picturing exactly that. "You have a problem."

"Yeah, I'm in the heart of Texas and not a cowboy in sight." She shook her head, those hazel eyes fixed on me. "It really is a travesty, Slayer."

I frowned. In Opey you couldn't toss a stone without hitting a cowboy, and that made me curious. "Doesn't Oakley have cowboys?"

"Not in my part of town." She shook it off and flashed a smile.

"We all work the ranch," I assured her. "Not always willingly, but when you're part of an organization, sometimes you have to do shit you don't want to do."

"No kidding," she said with a level of commiseration that gave me pause, which was saying a lot because every stroke of her fingertips came closer and closer to the tip of my semi-resting cock.

I laughed again, but this time it was a little mocking. "Yeah? What do you know about it, Ella Mae?"

Maybe it wrong to taunt her. Chance wasn't an airhead who'd just think it was a fun joke. She might stab my femoral artery before I realized I wasn't getting a blow job.

"A lot more than you think. Obviously." Her tone changed as much as her expression had, more serious and sober now instead of sated and flirtatious. She sat up, those beautiful tits on display and my mouth watered as my gaze lingered a second too long.

"There's no easy way to say it so I'm just gonna fuckin' blurt it out. I'm the VP of the Lords of Buckthorn MC."

It took a second to process her words because my mind was still laser focused on her tits, but eventually they sank in like a fucking ton of bricks. She was in a MC. Not a rival MC, but when it came to love, fucking, and romance it didn't matter. Another MC was another MC, and they didn't fucking mingle for more than a celebration.

"What did you just say?"

Chance sighed and dropped her hands into her lap, her gaze fixed on my face. "You heard me, Slayer."

"You're in an MC?" She nodded. "Not just someone's old lady or fuck toy?"

"Fuck you, and no. I'm the VP, like I said."

I couldn't believe it. Literally, I could not fucking believe it. My head wouldn't stop shaking. "Then you know exactly why this is a bad idea, Chance."

She nodded. "I wasn't asking you for a wedding ring, and I wasn't expecting to see you after that minute in the alley."

"It was more than a fucking minute," I growled.

She glared at me. "The point is that I wasn't expecting to see you after that and definitely not after that time in your house."

She was right, but that wasn't the fucking point. "You knew I was in a MC that night."

She nodded. "Not until we were too far in to stop, but yeah, I knew. It didn't matter because I wasn't trying to turn you into my man or anything, just a good, hard fuck."

Chance pushed off the bed, giving me a full view of her naked body in all its glory.

"Stop acting like I tried to trick you somehow."

"Didn't you?"

She barked out a laugh. "I tricked you into fucking me? Twice? Get over yourself Slayer. All I wanted was your cock."

"Yeah, well I hope it was memorable because it was the last fucking time, Chance. Goddammit! You know how fucked up this is?"

She nodded and dropped down on the bed with her back to me, long hair messy as it fell over her shoulders.

"Yeah, I know Slayer. Jesus fucking Christ, I know. I've heard it plenty of times," she groaned. "You live and die by your club."

"Mixing with another club will jeopardize that." It was something I assumed all clubs knew. It was a key to our survival.

"I know. I know."

"We can't do this again," I told her, my voice firm but almost panicked. I wanted to do it again and again but this was it. It had to be or we could face more shit than the MC had seen so far.

"I'm the one who told you this, but if it makes you feel better to think you ended things, go right ahead."

"That's not what this is about. What about your crazy ex. Is he a Buckthorn, too?"

"No. He's ex-MC."

I shook my head. "And you haven't fucked him up yet. Why?"

Chance glared at me with her hands on her hips, looking like a gorgeous warrior queen. "When you've got the weight of your MC on your back, Slayer, you can let me know."

WILD

"Bullshit. You're the VP, so you know better than me, or you should, the MC comes first. No matter what. You fucked up with your ex and now with me."

I shook my head, feeling something like loss as I shoved my feet into my jeans, quickly dressing and putting more and more distance between us.

"Get your shit together, Chance, before you end up dead."

"Thanks for the advice," she said, her voice condescending and bitter.

"I'm sorry about this, I really am. But the Reckless Bastards are who I am. They are my family and that oath means something to me. I can't, no I *won't* go back on that, no matter how good the pussy is."

"Somehow I'll survive without you." Her words were quiet and angry against my back, but I didn't look back and I didn't respond. I shoved my feet into my boots and got the fuck out of there.

Before I walked into more trouble.

Chapter Fourteen

Ella Mae

Being the lone woman in a motorcycle club was hard. Dating or fucking as the lone woman in an all-male organization with very strict rules was damn near impossible. And nothing highlighted that more than the way Slayer shot out of my place once I told him who I really was.

He was right to run. If I had more choices, I probably would have done what he did. Run like hell. But I didn't have more choices, and it was totally fucking unfair. Not that I was one of those naïve fools who believed in concepts like fairness. Life had done a good job of making damn sure I knew it was a fairytale, but this? It was just plain unfair.

The rest of my MC, for example, could go scratch an itch or get their dicks wet with any of the Ladies of Buckthorn or any fucking civilian in Texas. The same was true for Slayer, I was sure.

But me? Regular guys because they couldn't be called men by any stretch, were put off by a tough chick. The few who weren't were a little too fascinated. Men were fragile fucking creatures, which left me the option of traveling farther and farther away from home to find a decent dick, or my own hands and array of battery-operated boyfriends.

See? Un-fucking-fair.

But I knew that there was fuck all I could do about it. Slayer knew it too, which pissed me off even more now, nearly a week after he left skid marks in his hurry to get the fuck away from me. Not that I was still sore about it or anything.

I wasn't.

My pussy though, she was a little sad to see Slayer go. Okay, she was *a lot* sad to see that big sexy beast walk away. He had a body built to give a girl a good rough fuck and, man did he like hearing the sound of his name on my lips. Best of all, he worked harder and harder to make you scream his name, which only made me sadder that we couldn't even keep sleeping together.

"Finally," I groaned when the door to The Korean Cowboy opened and Curt walked in and joined me at my table where I was studying the menu.

"Did you forget the way to your favorite restaurant?"

He flashed a cocky grin that drew the attention of a table filled with too young cowgirls in skintight jeans. "Nah," he said, too distracted to look me in the eye.

That meant he was tied up with a woman, and I didn't want the details. "I already ordered. Sticky ginger ribs so you have time." I flashed a sweet smile and ignored the middle finger he aimed at me.

When the cute twenty-year-old waitress came to take our orders, Curt flirted with her shamelessly, and she flirted right back. But as soon as she was gone, he was all business again. "Feels good to be back home."

"It does." We were all back at the club house and tomorrow was our first meeting in the new and improved Lord's Lair. "The new security is impressive."

"That's what I was going for. Impressive and unobtrusive."

It was that. With motion sensors and cameras everywhere, there was no way in hell anyone could ever stage a surprise attack on us at home again.

I folded my arms on the table and leaned into to him. "So what's up?"

Curt shrugged, but he was shit at beating around the bush and worse at small talk. "I was hoping to get some Texas style Korean barbecue while you tell me your plan to handle Leon."

I leaned back and stared at him. "Who says I haven't dealt with him?" He hadn't been around in a while, but he wasn't gone. I knew that.

"If you had, you would have said something already and given us more of a reason to celebrate tomorrow." The bastard knew he was right. "So, Leon?"

"I haven't seen him in a week." I told him how things went down with us the last time. "That was the last time I saw him, and I haven't felt him following me." I wouldn't dare admit I was too distracted with personal matters to be completely sure, but I *was* reasonably sure. More than reasonably sure. I was sure.

Curt stared at me for a long time, that same thousand-yard stare that intimidated the fuck out of the guys. But it didn't do much for me.

"Bullshit, Chance. He's been hanging around all this time, all this *fucking* time, and then he just left because you stuck a blade to his throat? No fucking way."

He was probably right. "He's gone now, so what do you want me to do? Hunt him down and put a bullet in his head?"

WILD

"Yep. Make sure he's gone. For good this time, Chance."

"I will." I had to. This was on me, and I couldn't let Leon keep on harassing me and making the MC look bad. "I promise."

"I know," Curt said and dug into his mile-high pile of thin sliced beef. "Eat up, I got lunch plans."

I laughed and shook my head. "Didn't you just come from dinner plans?"

"Nope. Breakfast plans." The shit-eating grin he flashed told me everything I needed to know about his morning plans.

It kind of pissed me off all over again, thinking about how easily he and the others were able to get a little ass around here. My only hope at this point was to start wearing floral dresses and showing up at one of the two dozen churches in town on Sunday morning.

I snorted a laugh to myself. Like that would accomplish anything other than a wasted morning of discomfort. Not that my thoughts were all that comfortable right now anyway, bouncing from fairness to Slayer and back again. It was all one and the same in my mind, and I needed just stop thinking about it. There was nothing to do about it but put those memories in my flick bank and move on.

Curt wiped him mouth with a napkin and gave me a long look. "What's eatin' you Chance? You've been distracted lately."

I played with a forkful of barbecue. I didn't want to have this conversation. "I have not." I didn't *get* distracted, not how he meant. It was too dangerous, and I liked my danger controlled. "What have I missed, Curt? Have I screwed up anything? Forgotten anything?"

"Nothing. Shit, it's just a feeling I'm getting. You can talk to me, Chance."

If only he knew what was on my mind. But I couldn't let him in, couldn't tell him about Slayer. "I know. And if there was something to talk about, you are literally the only person I would come to."

He frowned. "Brick will be devastated to hear that."

"Doubtful."

Our plates were as empty as they would get and we stood, tossing a few bills on the table before we made our way out into the warm Texas sunshine. "What are you up to today, girl?"

"Don't know. Gonna go for a ride to clear my mind, see what's behind the fog."

"Enjoy. Stay safe." Curt hopped on his bike and took off one way, and I went the other, letting the open road soothe the rattled parts of me. The parts that were hesitant to deal with Leon because of our history, and the way he came back from his time in the Army a different man. The other parts of me that were totally fucking *shook* about the fact that I couldn't stop thinking about a certain long-haired biker.

What the fuck made Slayer so special? He was a man like any other. Expendable. Replaceable. Not remarkable, at least not beyond his size and his zest for pleasing a woman. After Leon, I promised myself I wouldn't get lost in a man—would never ever get so wrapped up in a man or a relationship that I forgot who the fuck I was.

And look at me.

A half dozen or more incredible, really fucking incredible, orgasms later, and I'm looking for ways to keep fucking him. Like a fiend.

Am I any better than Leon?

Maybe not, but there was a big difference between us. I was trying to fight it. Hard. Leon seemed to want to lean into the bad shit.

"Speak of the fucking devil." An hour of pavement was behind me and I'd started to relax, enjoying the miles upon miles of farms and ranches, cows, horses and even a few goats as the land flew by.

But my mistake—again—was relaxing. A blue and orange bike had been behind me for the past few miles, but I didn't think anything of it since we hadn't passed any exits. Yet.

But now, two exits later, and I'd recognize that wobbly lane change anywhere. Leon. He used to be one of the best riders I'd ever seen, flashy and capable, making even his big cumbersome Harley seem lightweight. If I hadn't been so busy climbing the MC ladder, maybe I would have seen that getting rid of the big Harley in favor of a sportier style was the beginning of the end.

Now he was less than ten feet behind me, and there was no goddamn way I could relax with Leon so close. I pulled over at the empty rest stop that still showed signs of ongoing construction. I parked my bike and removed my helmet before Leon could do the same.

I glared at him with my nastiest side eye. "Leon, what the fuck?"

He flashed a lopsided smile but it didn't reach his bloodshot eyes that were the size of pinpricks. Deep purple skin formed craters under his eyes. His clothes were dirty and slept in, but he kept that smile in place. "Hey babe," he said in a voice meant to be sexy but grated on me like fingernails on a chalkboard.

"Don't fucking *hey babe* me, Leon. Why are you following me?"

"Was I? I thought we were going for a ride."

"What the fuck are you smoking?" I held up a hand. "Actually, I don't want to know."

He pulled his leg across his bike and strolled toward me, ignoring the way I stepped back and gripped my helmet just a little tighter.

"Come on baby, don't be like that. I've missed you." His lips puckered and I took another step back when I caught a whiff of his day-old breath.

"God, I've missed your body," he said. "Those tits."

He reached out and moved so fast that before I knew it, he actually squeezed my left breast. My helmet flew up as if it had a mind of its own. It smashed the side of his head and sent him to his knees.

I pointed one finger at him. "Don't. Fucking. Touch. Me." I glared with all the hate I could muster just to make sure he got the point. Clearly.

"I've tried real hard, Leon, to respect what we once were to each other. And every fucking day you make me regret it. Guess what? I'm done."

He was just some guy making trouble for the MC. No more. No less.

"You don't mean that."

I absolutely did, and I nodded to let him know I meant business. I reached behind me until I felt the cool handle of my favorite piece and wrapped my hands around it.

"I do mean it, Leon. You made your choices, and I've made mine."

It would be so easy to just end it right here and toss him in a dumpster. It'd take some time on my own, but there were no people or cameras around.

"You chose the MC." He said each word like it was a curse, spitting them at me.

"I did. You didn't."

Just as I pulled the gun free, an eighteen-wheeler pulled in. Ruining the moment.

"Now it's time we both start living with the consequences of our choices, Leon. Leave Oakley, in fact, leave Texas altogether."

He shook his head and stood up, legs still wobbly. "I won't ever leave, Chance, not without you. You're mine. Forever."

I glared at him and backed up until I was at my bike.

"That's where you're wrong Leon. One way or the other you *will* leave Oakley." We stared at each other for a long minute, a million different conversations going on in that extended moment that said so much, pleading and begging on both our parts. Memories. Love. Fights. Hate. The drugs.

"I guess we'll see about that."

We wouldn't see about a damn thing. I got on my bike and headed home where there was wine, pizza and Netflix waiting for me. Next time I saw Leon, things wouldn't go so well for him.

Chapter Fifteen

Slayer

"Peaches find anything yet?" I stood in the middle of the kitchen, heavy-lidded eyes on Gunnar's face with my arms crossed.

He shook his head, but it was the woman herself who spoke. "Peaches is *right here,* and of course I found something. Who do you think I am?"

I shrugged and dragged my feet over to the coffee pot, desperately in need of Martha's special blend of strong, black and bitter.

"I think you're a computer genius, Peaches, but you haven't said anything so I figured...never mind."

"Figured what? Say it." She motioned for me to speak my mind and instead I took a long sip of the piping hot liquid, letting it slide down my throat. I gave it a few seconds, hoping the jolt of energy I craved would come faster only because I needed it to. "Go on," she insisted.

"I figured you'd want me to talk to Big Poppa." I practically spit out my coffee, but the deranged look on her face was well worth it.

"You have a death wish?" She flashed an evil smile that said payback was a bitch. "Big Poppa my ass. Rocco McNally. Born and raised in the state of Washington. Recently divorced after a decade of marriage. Works as an accountant at a marketing firm. No criminal record."

"None?" My gaze went to Gunnar, confusion swimming in my eyes because I swore he told me his mom got around. A lot.

"Some seemingly stand up guys pay for it too, Slayer," he spat the words at me, angry. "She said she had no clue. Begged me not to judge her, so I didn't. Why should we even believe this motherfucker?"

"I don't believe him at all, but he knows he's risking life and limb to get this close, which means *he* believes it. Maybe we ought to find out why."

It was harder to convince people that they believed something wrong than anything else, which meant we had our work cut out for us.

"Anything else, Peaches?"

She shook her head, copper curls flying, her movements jostled Stone awake. "None. No debt. No trouble. Just a boring old dude who wants me to kick his ass for trying to take my girl away."

Though she hadn't given birth to Maisie, Peaches protected her just as if she had.

That's the part that worried me. I said, "I can go take care of this right now. Say the word Gunnar."

"I appreciate it, Slayer, but we have to face it. Eventually."

"I hear you. I fucking hate it, but I hear you." That didn't mean I would take this lying down though. "Anyway we can dirty him up just in case we need to?"

Peaches leaned forward and patted my cheek. "I love the way you think sometimes. It's too bad you're such a slut, or I'd spend my free time finding you a woman."

She had no way of knowing just how much her words had conjured up the image of a certain dark-haired beauty with a potty mouth and a sinful body. "I don't need a woman."

Especially one with ties to another MC. That shit was a big no-no and there was nothing in the world good enough for the kind of shit that could bring.

Peaches snorted a laugh and took a sip of juice with an exaggerated sigh. "Your mouth says one thing, but your eyes say another. It's okay, I'm patient."

"Crazy, that's what you are. Instead of matchmaking, let's find out everything there is to know about Rocco. Even reaching out to the former Mrs. McNally if we need to."

"Let's see if we need to first," Gunnar added, amusement sparkling in his eyes. "Isn't it your day off?"

I nodded. "And?"

"And usually you're balls deep in some woman this time of day," Peaches added with a smirk. "Are you on antibiotics, or do you want to watch the little guy so I can have some grownup time with my man?"

Ugh, that was the last fucking thing I wanted to think about, no matter how hot Peaches was. "I might have said yes, but now I have to book an appointment to scrub my brain of the last fifteen seconds."

"Very funny." She stood and put Stone in my arms, the cute little fucker looked up with a wet grin, two little teeth sticking out.

"Maybe a little baby time is just what you need to remind you what could happen with all those ladies hanging off of you."

I shook my head and laughed. "I'm always safe. Always." Except there was a time in the very recent past where I wasn't as careful as I usually was. Several times, in fact.

"All it takes is one time. One little sperm and *bam*, a little Slayer on the way by Random Barbie No. 283432." She flashed a grin and stroked my beard in a gesture so motherly it could have been Martha doing it.

"Thanks for taking the little guy, Slayer."

How did this happen exactly? "Where's Maisie?" I asked to change the subject.

"Sleepover with the Sheriff's granddaughter," she said and headed out of the kitchen with a smile, Gunnar at her feet. Then they were both gone, and it was just me and Stone and my wayward thoughts.

No, not wayward thoughts. More like reckless thoughts, because that's what they were. Any and all thoughts of Chance were reckless because they only made me want what I couldn't have. What I knew I couldn't have. And that just pissed me off. A full week since I left her bed, and sometimes I swear I could still smell her scent on me, hear the way she moaned when I licked her. The way her eyes lit up when she sucked me off. It was bad.

Really fucking bad.

No woman was worth this amount of head space, especially one who already belonged to another MC. Okay she didn't *belong* to them, she wasn't anybody's old lady, but that just made it worse. She was all the way in, committed. Loyal. There was nothing to be done about it so I needed to just fucking stop.

It was a fucked up situation, and the worst part of all was that I just couldn't stop thinking about her. Chance. Ella Mae.

Whatever her name was, I pushed it and her face and her body, far from my mind.

Stone made some incoherent baby noises to draw my attention, and I smiled down at him.

"What I need is the perfect distraction." And as soon as grownup time was over, I'd head to one of the bars in the area and find a woman to warm my bed for the rest of the night.

Chapter Sixteen

Ella Mae

"I don't know, Toni, maybe we should just go somewhere else?"

I sat in my friend Antonia's car outside The Barn Door, my heart thudding in my chest, and my stomach doing somersaults behind my barely there masquerade-themed outfit.

Toni nodded and handed me her favorite leather and rhinestone-studded flask.

"I'm totally sure. This worked out perfectly. You can get over the mystery man you refuse to talk about with someone new, and I can find some sexy cougar to lick me until Dex shows up!"

Antonia used to be one of the Ladies of Buckthorn with hopes of being made someone's old lady but it never happened. She fell in love with a civilian and our friendship was all that remained of her time with the Lords of Buckthorn.

I laughed at her excitement. "You guys *do* like to keep things interesting, don't you?"

"You have no idea, Ella! Two kids with all kinds of activities and obligations. Yeah, we try to enjoy ourselves when we can." She tossed her blonde hair back and laughed. "I can't wait to see who Dex shows up as tonight!"

I rolled my eyes. "Is there such a thing as too much role playing?"

"Not when you're at risk of losing yourself in the roles of wife and mother. Tonight I get to be young-ish, sexy and wild. A woman. *Just* a horny fucking woman."

It was more the look in her eyes than her tone that sold me. I nodded my agreement.

"All right. We're already here and you're right, this might be the best place for me."

A sex club was never something I would have considered. Not because I was a prude or anything, but because I didn't need a lot of kink to get off. I appreciated a bit of spanking, choking, and hair pulling. Hell, I'd even let Leon tie me up a time or two, but it wasn't necessary, so I kept my distance. But tonight I would keep an open mind.

"You mean Mr. Unforgettable *didn't* rock your world and ruin you for future men?"

She arched a blonde brow at me and puckered her hot pink lips before turning to the mirror to put on her mask. The theme tonight was Kinky Masquerade, and we both dressed the part.

"He totally rocked my world but he's not an option."

I'd dedicated more of my free time to finding a loophole than I would ever admit to anyone, but I had. One final idea was playing around in my mind, but it sounded insane to me so saying it out loud wasn't an option. *Yet.*

"Then I'm really fuckin' sorry it didn't work out, Ella. But if anyone can find a way, it's you."

I appreciated her saying, so but it was time to give up that idea, even if I *was* playing with fire by messing around in Slayer's backyard.

"Do you think the peacock and black feathers are too much?"

I arched a brow at Toni and laughed. "You're asking the woman in all white with red fucking feathers? I'm not sure which of us is crazier."

She laughed again and we got out of the car, shook our feathers, and hooked our sparkly purses over our shoulders. Toni wrapped her arm in mine as we made our way to the door. "Who gives a shit, babe? We're looking hot as shit, we're gonna get tipsy as fuck and bang out some orgasms tonight. Right?" She held up her fist with a stubborn look on her face.

"Fuckin' A right," I told her and bumped her fist.

"That's my girl."

After an easy but surprisingly high-tech entrance, we were inside the club. The lights were dim and the music was loud. Really fucking loud and pumping an electronic beat mixed with some kind of classical music. It should've been fucking offensive, but it kind of worked, thanks to the steady throbbing beat that made me want to move my hips.

This place didn't look like it was run by bikers and definitely not a bunch of military vets. The whole décor was true to theme, dark and sexy, but right out of those BBC period dramas, if they aired on a porn channel.

"This place is…wow." I couldn't keep the surprise out of my voice.

"I know, right?" Toni had to shout over the music as we pushed up to the bar. "What are you drinking?"

I looked at the specials and howled. "I'll have the Wet Knickers."

WILD

She laughed. "If you're lucky, you'll lose 'em altogether."

I shook my head at her joke, but I kept my head moving because my pulse had kicked up and my skin heated up. Not a lot, but just enough to notice. "If I lose them in this outfit they'll toss me in jail."

"I'll pay your bail."

"Thanks." I took the colorful drink and followed Toni since this was her turf. Tonight, I was her guest, but she and Dex came often because they could play out their fantasies safely. And without risk of kids interrupting.

"Look around. See what you like."

I was already doing that because, unlike a nightclub, there was plenty of walking room even though the place was packed. Beds, platforms, ottomans, stools, pillows, booths, and even tables served as an acceptable surface for all types of freaky-deaky. Nothing was taboo as long as it was consensual, and so far, The Barn Door was an 'anything goes' kind of place. And I was intrigued. This place might be just what I needed.

"I'm looking."

"Evening ladies."

A woman with curly pink hair, shiny natural lips, and an impressive set of cleavage stopped in front of us with a smile. The one for me was polite, but when she looked at Toni there was hunger.

"I was just telling my wife how tasty you looked. She agreed."

Toni was powerless to suppress the shiver that went through her at the thought of two tongues on her, and I knew she was a goner. When it came to getting her pussy licked, the woman was like a kid in a candy store.

"Catch ya later, Chance."

I shook my head with a smile, almost envious of Antonia's love of men and women. My life would be a hell of a lot easier if I could just be happy with what was around. But when I got to the bottom level of the club and the music was still loud but no longer deafening, I felt myself relax. There was a dark eroticism about this area. The hall was dim but looked safe and the sounds of sex, of fucking, of pleasure echoed from every room I passed.

The first room I passed was decorated for romance and two dudes were in the middle of a hot sixty-nine that got me a little hot. Two young dudes full of muscles wore leather hoods as they shoved their tongues deep inside a redheaded MILF with her head thrown back, a look of pure bliss on her face. *Lucky bitch*. In the next room a couple did a bunch of S&M shit I'd never seen before, and I watched out of curiosity before moving on. To the orgy room.

I stepped inside right away, glancing at the nine people touching and tasting and fucking each other on a floor covered in about a thousand pillows in different colors and sizes. It was pleasure over pleasure, the scent of sweat and sex in the air, moans and sights swirling in the air. I had to squeeze my knees together to stop the flow of desire.

I took a step forward and an arm snaked around my waist and pulled me back, against a hard wide chest. A familiar scent. A more familiar erection pressed against my ass.

"Chance."

Slayer. I *knew* he was there even though I hadn't spotted him anywhere. I felt him, and now he was here, warm breath fanning my neck, heartbeat pulsing against my back.

"That's me," I managed to choke out, working hard to hide my surprise. I knew there was a chance I'd run into him, and I thought I was ready for it.

I wasn't.

"It's you," he whispered in my ear and there was fuck all I could do to stop the shiver he produced. He chuckled and the sound vibrated through me, stopping at my clit. I gasped when his hips ground against me, allowing me another feel of his cock.

With the feel his of his big body, his shallow breaths behind me, and all the fucking going on in front of me, I was ready to fuck. Slayer's big hands slid up my hips and up, stopping to cup my tits.

"Fuck, I've missed these. Last night I dreamed I slid my cock between them and right into your mouth."

Oh fuck. "Did you?" My words were breathless, and I didn't give a shit. I was past the point of pretending this wasn't gonna happen.

He growled. "Not here." Before I could ask what he meant, Slayer had tightened his grip around my waist and lifted me off the ground, carrying me down the hall to a locked room. It looked ominous but he moved smoothly, producing a key to unlock the door, yanking it open and then locking us inside.

He set me down, and I looked around. The room was painted black or maybe it was a deep blue or purple. Either way, it was dark and the satin bedding on the bed in the middle of the room was all black. It was dark. Intense. Kind of fucking hot.

"Colorful."

"Private."

Right. Because no one could see us.

"Even better."

Slayer's lips curled into a grin, and damn, I felt it deep inside of me, like a flicker of a flame. He lifted me in the air once again, brushing his lips over my cleavage once again before tossing me on the all-black bed. He looked me over for a long time, and I wondered if he was debating whether or not to go through with this. Desire burned in his eyes and his cock was fighting to get out of his pants.

"This is a bad idea."

I nodded. "Probably."

Slayer dropped to his knees and parted mine with his hands, running those big hands up my bare thighs until his thumbs ghosted over my pussy.

"A really bad idea."

"Terrible," I agreed and tossed my head back when one thumb found my clit.

The sound of my panties tearing came next and then a moan that slipped from my lips as his tongue found my opening.

Slayer growled. "I don't give a fuck."

He waited, his breath coming out in sharp hot pants against my wet pussy, and I shivered as I looked down at him, knowing he wanted me to say I didn't give a fuck either. Instead I smiled.

"I guess how I feel about this will depend on how happy I am when we're done."

Slayer's grin was a thing of beauty. When he flashed it while his tongue curled around my clit, I was in heaven.

"Then I guess I better make sure you have a good time."

That was the only thing guaranteed tonight anyway.

Chapter Seventeen

Slayer

I knew the moment Chance walked into the club because I felt it. Felt *her*. I didn't spot her right away, not with all the fucking masks everyone wore. It made security a nightmare, and I did not envy Ford tonight.

At all.

Then I spotted her with a blonde chick, both of them wearing masks with three fucking feet of feathers sticking out of their heads. It looked ridiculous, but her outfit was hot as fuck. It was barely there but somehow prim and out of character for the Chance I knew. Maybe there was something to this Kinky Masquerade idea that Hennessy put together after all.

I couldn't take my eyes off her, and when a couple of our regulars scooped up her friend, I followed Chance downstairs at a discreet distance. I didn't believe Chance was here to fuck with me or to get me to reconsider. She would have been here a lot sooner if she'd planned to do that, which meant she was here to fuck someone else.

And that shit burned my inside like lava.

I didn't know if it was jealousy or just macho bullshit, and I didn't care. The minute she stepped into the orgy room with too much curiosity on her face, I knew how this night would play out.

I knew I'd take her to the black room where we could have absolute privacy. I knew I'd take this one little indulgence because I wanted her, and the universe had tossed her in my path. Again. It was piss poor reasoning, but the sound of my name on her lips made it all worth it.

"Slayer, fuck! Yes! Oh fuck yes!" I smiled against her pussy, wet and creamy as she tightened her thighs around my head as her orgasm worked its way up her body. I loved how vocal Chance was, how she wasn't afraid to say what she liked. And what she didn't.

"More. Yes. Oh fuck, just like tha-at!"

Her breaths came out short and choppy and her thighs tightened so hard my ears began to ring. Then the orgasm released her and jerked her about. My tongue kept a steady torture on her clit while she pulsed around two of my fingers.

"I love watching you come."

She gave me a sleepy and erotic grin and it was pure fucking satisfaction.

"You're so fucking good at that," she panted. "So good I'd pay for it, but I want more. I need more Slayer."

"My fingers are still inside of you."

"I know," she said and pulsed around them with a groan. "And now I'm ready for that big cock of yours."

Coming from another woman it might seem like needless flattery, but from Chance it was just a fact as she saw it. I stood slowly and removed my fingers from her body, and Chance slid to the floor with a wicked grin, hands working quickly to release my cock from my jeans.

"Chance," I growled when she squeezed my cock.

"Yes?" She flicked her gaze up to me and licked me from the underside of my balls to the tip of my cock, all the way around until I was so hard my cock ached. She slid her lips around the tip and took me deeper and deeper until I hit the back of her throat and she moaned. *She* fucking moaned.

"Chance," I growled and tossed her on the bed once again, this time there was no teasing, no playing around. I pushed her thighs open with one hand and guided my cock into her still pulsing pussy. "Oh fuck. Chance," I moaned.

"Fuck, right?" She looked up at me a dark look in her eyes and a slow grin on her lips as she fell back against the bed and wrapped her legs around my waist. "You feel so fucking good, Slayer."

She felt good but hearing her say it in that dark, satisfied tone felt even fucking better. I held her, close and tight, and thrust into her over and over again. I didn't want to rush it, knowing this was it, so I took my time. Slow dragging strokes that went on and on, denying us both the pleasure of a quick and powerful orgasm.

She was beautiful with her hair wild and spilling everywhere, her body coated in a fine sheen of sweat, her skin hot from exertion while she continued to cling to me. To beg. "Slayer, please."

"Not. Yet." The words came out on a growl, and I let one hand slide up and down her body while the other found her clit. Flicked it over and over as each and every one of her muscles tightened, one by one.

"Slayer."

Fuck, that sound never got old. I flicked harder and faster but my strokes stayed the same even as she bucked harder to get closer.

"Wait," I said.

"I. Can't." Whatever she was about to say next had been cut off by a powerful orgasm that took her by surprise and shook her violently. She squeezed and clenched my cock in a tight fist that unlocked my own orgasm.

We bucked and shouted our pleasure together. Simultaneously. I held her tight while my hips worked out the last of my pleasure, extending her own.

"Fuck. I can't feel my legs," I snorted on a laugh.

Chance shivered and giggled before laughter erupted from her, loud and throaty. Sexy. Her hands snaked down my back, and she squeezed my ass while her feet danced along the backs of my thighs.

"I feel them just fine. Firm. Muscular."

I laughed and rolled off her. "What are you doing later?" The question popped out before I could filter it. Stop it.

She blinked up at me and tried to hide her confused frown. "Uhm, nothing, I guess. Going home."

In for a penny, as they say. "Meet me at my place later?"

It took just a minute, but then she nodded, and I leaned over her, kissing her one more time since I was officially still on the clock. I couldn't help it, two of my fingers found their way inside her slick cunt and pulled a low moan from her. Chance grabbed my wrist and ground against me with a moan and rode out the last of her aftershocks. Fucking gorgeous.

"I can't fucking wait," I told her and took a step back, licking my fingers clean before I got dressed and left before I locked us in there forever.

Chapter Eighteen

Ella Mae

"I can't get enough of you."

Slayer's growled those words in my ear, his big hands squeezing my tits as his hot orgasm pumped into my body. The words were nice, the orgasm was amazing.

"Good to know," I told him and pushed back against him so that I had all of him to squeeze as my own orgasm pumped out of me.

"Good morning," I said, smiling the last of my release.

Slayer chuckled and the sound skittered over my bare flesh, making me shiver. And smile.

"Good morning. Again."

Sometime around three in the morning Slayer drove me home in hopes that no one would see us together, and if they did, they wouldn't recognize us in a nondescript navy blue pickup truck. Then, instead of driving back to Hardtail Ranch, he'd come inside.

Several times.

"Better than any alarm clock," I told him and turned on my back when he slipped from my body. "Yes," I groaned when he wrapped his mouth around my nipple.

"Good to know." His lips found that spot between my neck and my shoulder and the kiss almost brought a tear to my eye. Thankfully, Slayer put some distance between us by getting off the bed. And then more when he started to dress.

"This shouldn't have happened."

It was just like a man to ruin a perfect moment by opening his mouth.

"Save it Slayer. I know it as well as you do but it happened anyway."

And even though I wished it was different, I didn't think it was possible.

"I didn't hold a gun to your head, so you can save your speech."

"I know. I didn't mean it like that dammit." He raked a hand through his long thick hair, tangled from hours of my hands playing in those soft locks. He finished dressing, and I watched, ogled really, because he was a work of art.

"I have to go," he said, and I detected a note of disappointment that matched my own.

"I know."

Slayer nodded and walked around the bed, laying his big body on top of mine so his denim covered cock brushed right against my bare pussy. I moaned, and he grinned, brushing a soft kiss over my lips.

"Later."

He left, leaving me to ponder whether that was an empty promise or one he planned to fulfill. Only time would tell, and it wouldn't matter if I didn't talk to Curt.

Soon.

And handle Leon.

Sooner.

After a quick nap, I got up and showered, popped a load of laundry into the wash, and did all the things I neglected to do during the week. I basically wasted time until it was late enough to show up at the clubhouse and catch Curt alone.

He was saying goodbye to his latest overnight guest when I pulled into the parking lot. I had to grin at the speed Curt went through women.

"See you soon Alina."

"Breaking hearts this early in the morning?"

He grinned at me and held the door open. "Maybe breaking a bed or two but no hearts were involved. What brings you by so early?"

"I was hoping we could talk."

Curt nodded, giving away nothing of his emotions as he poured two cups of coffee. "You gettin' cold feet when it comes to Leon?"

I shook my head. "Fuck no. My resolve is strong on that front. You were right about him, about everything, and I'm working on it."

"So what's this about?"

I sighed because I hadn't really imagined I'd get to the point where he'd actually listen.

"Okay, the thing is we need numbers, Curt. Right now, there are only five of us but Bones hasn't really been involved in a while, and that brings us down to four. If some shit kicks off with the cartel again, or the next MC who wants to show us how big their dicks are, we're fucked."

Curt's nostrils flared at talk of the Mexican cartel. We lost a couple of guys and spent a fucking fortune on the new clubhouse. It was a sore spot for him. "You ain't tellin' me anything I don't already know, Chance."

"What if we explore the idea of a brotherhood of sorts, alliances if that word makes you feel better. We partner with other MCs on an as needed basis to get rid of a common enemy or as backup when needed. For cash or guns or whatever deals are made."

My heart raced as I tried to recall all the details I'd come up with last night between rounds of intense fucking with Slayer. Curt needed to know everything on my mind.

"The Lords will always be our top priority, but until we do some recruitment, we'd have numbers when we need them."

Curt nodded absently, but I could see the gears turning in his head. I already knew a few of the questions he would ask.

"This about that man with the Reckless Bastards?"

I nodded because Curt and I had been through too much to start lying to each other now.

"In part, but it's also because they are the Opey, TX chapter and already have ties to their parent club in Vegas."

His eyes went wide at that bit of information.

"You've been busy."

"You made some good points about Leon, and I realized I spent too much fucking time reacting to him and stopped putting the club first. Stopped thinking about my duty as VP."

"Can't say I don't love to hear that."

"I'll focus on recruitment once Leon is handled. He's not exactly the billboard we want to advertise."

Curt snorted. "No shit."

"A lot of details would have to be settled," I warned him.

"I know. Talk to the Reckless Bastards to see if they'd consider it and be sure you let them know that we're small but powerful."

I grinned. "What else would I tell them?"

"Lords for Life."

"Lords for Life," I echoed back, feeling lighter as I finished my coffee.

It couldn't really be that easy, could it?

Chapter Nineteen

Slayer

"Slayer, you have a visitor."

Ford's deep voice sounded in my earpiece. Saint insisted we all wear one after the last time someone snuck a gun inside the club. The suicide was bad press, and it had taken a shit ton of work to lure all the members back. Though it felt like we were all still on active duty, it made communicating in the big ass club a hell of a lot easier.

"Send them downstairs," I told Ford.

Women always thought showing up at the club would get my attention and plenty of them went to great, kinky lengths to get it.

"No can do. Not a member and not a guest." Ford's tone was all business and that put me on edge.

"On my way," I told him and squared my shoulders as I climbed the staircase and headed for the exit. I hoped it was Rocco because I could use a face to pound the shit out of right about now. I hadn't seen or heard from Chance, and I didn't expect to, but dammit I really wanted to.

"Ladies." I tipped my imaginary hat at three women who'd just entered wearing little more than lingerie.

"Dayum! I hope to see *you* later," one of them said, making the other two giggle like schoolgirls.

When they were inside and headed toward one of the bars, I stepped out and looked to Ford. And then...

"Chance? What are you doing here?"

She nibbled her lip in a sexy yet vulnerable move she would never do if she knew how unsure she looked.

"I told him I would wait until you were done."

I looked to Ford and he nodded, confirming her words.

"Okay well I'm here now. What's up?"

Ford cleared his throat. "Fifteen minutes until closing if you want to stand outside and keep an eye on anyone who shouldn't be driving home?"

I made a note to myself to get the kid a big bottle of his favorite tequila when he officially became one of us.

"Thanks man. Come on." We stepped just outside the doors and around the corner, giving me a good view of both parking areas.

"What's up?"

"I don't know how much you know about my club, the Lords, but lately our numbers are down."

"Yeah, I heard you had some shit with the Mexican Devils." They'd set their club house on fire too. "You handled them well."

"Thanks. But we still lost two brothers, and our numbers are too low to be as effective as we need."

I nodded, listening out of curiosity because the Reckless Bastards weren't all that large either.

"What are you getting at?"

"An alliance of sorts," she began, and I listened to her talk about helping each other keep our small towns safe.

"We've found that keeping the shit out of town means they look the other way when they can."

"Us too," I agreed. I watched more and more members spill into the parking lot, making plans for later tonight or saying goodbye until next time they were ready for a good fuck

"My Prez, Curt, is interested if your Prez is too. It could help us both until we have bigger numbers."

It was a damn good idea, and it would've been nice to have more numbers to have Peaches' back, or to handle that old Irish motherfucker that brought Hennessy to Hardtail Ranch.

"I'll have to talk to my Prez, Gunnar, about it first, but I'll let you know."

"Really?"

I nodded and licked my lips as I pushed off the building and leaned in real close.

"Yeah, and I'm flattered you'd go through all this just to have me again."

She gave me a long hard stare and then burst out laughing. "The dick is good, but this is business, Slayer."

"Business that'll allow us to keep fucking if we want to?"

"Like I said, *mutually beneficial*." She grinned and licked her lips and dammit, I couldn't help it, I leaned in for a taste myself. Her lips were lush and plump, tasted like that fucking fruity gum she liked to chew.

"It's been too fucking long," I growled against her lips. She leaned into me, flung her arms around my neck and purred.

WILD

"Not too long. Your mouth was just on me. This morning. In the shower."

I growled and pulled her closer, deepening the kiss, but Chance pulled back and I frowned. "What the hell?"

She nodded to the parking lot. "Aren't you still working?"

Only two cars were still in the lot and one belonged to Ford.

"Shit. See what you do to me woman?"

She was a hella distraction, dammit, one I couldn't afford. Maybe this damn alliance would be what I needed to work her out of my system.

"What do I do to you Slayer?" She pressed against me and jumped back when the front door banged open.

Ford and Saint walked out first and Hazel came out last, locking the doors and setting the alarm. Tomorrow a cleaning crew would come in and work their magic and we'd come in to change it all up once again.

"You still here?"

I nodded at Saint's question and ignored the smirk on his face.

"Helping Ford out here. Only sober drivers pulled out. You know who's car that is?" I pointed a thumb over my shoulder just as a gunshot rang out, echoing in the air. We fell to the ground instinctively, me and Ford anyway. Saint fell on top of Hazel and that was when I heard a scream. A woman's scream.

"Chance!"

"Shit. Shit. I'm hit," she groaned and fell to the ground. I was at her side in an instant, my hand over the blood spreading out on the left side of her midsection.

"Shooter. By. White. Car."

"White car," I yelled out and applied more pressure to her wound. I heard the footsteps more than saw them or were aware of them, but I knew Ford and Saint were armed. They would handle whoever was crazy enough to shoot at the Reckless Bastards.

"Ella!"

I looked up at the voice and saw a familiar face.

"What the fuck are you doing here?"

It was Chance's ex, Leon. The fucker who shot her.

"I'll kill you, piece of shit!" I lunged at him, but Chance's lightweight grip on my hand stopped me.

WILD

"We got 'em," Ford said, both he and Saint had their guns trained on the asshole. Hazel, I guessed was calling in backup.

"Ella, I'm sorry. I didn't mean to shoot you baby, I didn't." There was no doubt that his emotions were real, but that didn't change a damn thing.

"You. Fucking. Shot. Me." Her words came out on harsh, difficult breaths. The pain and blood loss affecting her.

"I meant to shoot this asshole with his hands all over you! You're mine baby, can't you see we belong together?"

She shook her head, skin pale and sweaty. "We. Don't. Leon."

"Of course, I fucking changed. I killed kids, Ella Mae. Kids! You know what that does to a man?"

The gun in his hand flung wildly, but for now he wasn't aiming it at anyone.

"I know. Tried to be there. Resented me."

"You became VP of MY fucking club. What else was I supposed to do?"

"Support. Me."

His shoulders fell at her words, and Leon nodded. "I'm sorry baby. For everything. Forgive me?"

"Leave." Her breathing was coming in shallow, and she was losing too much blood.

"Come with me, Ella. We can start over some place new. Just the two of us."

She smiled, and shook her head. "Kill. Him."

The hope in Leon's eyes faded, and he lifted the gun.

"Put it down," Saint shouted, gun aimed at Leon's chest.

"You'll kill me anyway," he said and put the barrel under his chin. He pulled the trigger and fell to the ground.

When I turned back, Chance's eyes were closed, and I hoped for her sake, she had passed out before seeing that motherfucking coward die.

Chapter Twenty

Ella Mae

"You want to talk about this shit now? Right now?"

I didn't know who the angry man posing the question was, but his deep and growly voice was the first thing I heard when I woke up. In a semi-panic. I knew some shit had gone down because the last thing I remember was pressing up against Slayer's big hard body, and the pain on my left side was too fucking familiar.

I was shot. And the growly voiced man sounded angry and frustrated, but he also sounded afraid. Or concerned.

"I'd say right now is a good fucking time to talk about it. When else you wanna do it? When we're neck deep in shit with no plan to get out of it?"

That no-nonsense voice mixed with a heavy dose of sarcasm was Slayer's. That meant I was probably somewhere on Hardtail Ranch. I kept my eyes closed to see if I could hear anything beyond the men on the other side of what I assumed was the door. I didn't know yet because opening my eyes took some effort. More effort than I could muster up at the moment.

I squeezed my eyes shut and tried to sit up, hoping it would force my eyes open. All it did was send an ugly moan shooting between my lips. The door flew open and, what do you know, it opened my eyes right up. Defense mechanism, I supposed. But it was temporary because the next moment my eyes slammed shut on a moan, and I fell back against a stack of pillows.

The first voice to speak surprised me. It was soft and feminine.

"How are you feeling?"

I snorted at her question. "Like I got a shot of lead. How's it look?"

It hurt like hell, but it felt like it was clean and bandaged, if not stitched.

"My head hurts like a motherfucker."

Two snorts, both of them masculine sounding and slowly my eyes opened on a pretty brunette with red glasses.

"You got a pretty good bump when you hit the ground. Now that you're up, I'll give you a quick concussion test."

"You a doctor or what?"

She smiled and nodded. "Yes, I'm a doctor. Call me Annabelle."

"Thanks, Annabelle. Where am I?"

"Gunnar's house on Hardtail Ranch." Slayer's deep voice was on my other side but I didn't turn, not yet. I couldn't. I didn't know why, but I kept my gaze on the doctor.

"Where's my phone?" I said. I was sure I sounded groggy as shit, but I needed to call Curt. I wasn't sure what had happened or who'd witnessed it, but the last thing the Lords needed was trouble with another MC.

"I need my phone."

"Need to check on Leon?"

Finally, my gaze swung to Slayer at his jealous and inappropriate comment. I glared. Hard.

"What? I need my phone. If my Prez hears about this he'll assume the worst."

I sat up, and Annabelle put a hand on my shoulder to stop me.

"We'll give your phone when your head is clear. Now stay calm or you'll pop those stitches. It'll hurt more with you conscious." Her words stopped me cold. Unconscious. I'd been shot, of course, but unconscious?

"Pain or blood loss?"

She shrugged and cast a quick look at Slayer and Gunnar.

"A little of both I would guess. It took some time to get to you."

Her words were ominous, but I suddenly understood.

"Take it easy, Chance. You're young and healthy. If you do what I say, you'll heal with no problem. Probably not even a scar."

"Thanks. And thank you for not calling the cops." Annabelle's grin was tight, and when I tried to swallow there was sand instead of saliva.

"We haven't decided that yet." Gunnar, I assumed.

"That's what we were discussing when you woke up," Slayer said, his gaze fixed angrily on his president. He turned to the doctor, his face softening to a friendly smile.

"Give us a minute AB? Then you can have all the time you need with the patient."

"Sure." She turned to me. "Calm."

"Got it."

WILD

"Five minutes," she said with a pointed look at Gunnar, recognizing him as the authority in this room. I wondered how on earth she got twisted up with an MC.

"No more. She needs to rest."

As soon as she was gone, Slayer turned to me. "Chance, this is Gunnar, the President of the Reckless Bastards, Opey Texas Chapter."

Oh so formal.

Another man, with dark hair and gorgeous blue eyes to match his handsome face, walked in. He looked like every girl's bad boy fantasy. And that black clove cigarette hanging out of his mouth was a picture in itself. He grinned.

"I think you make him nervous."

I frowned, feeling like I'd missed a thread in the conversation.

The blue-eyed bad boy spoke up. "You said *oh, so formal.*" Then added with a smirk, "AB must have given you the good stuff."

"Who are you?"

"Wheeler. VP."

"Nice to meet you. And you're Gunnar. I think."

Wheeler snickered again. "What's up?"

Gunnar sucked in a deep breath that threatened to steal all the air from the room.

"I just don't get why we need to even discuss this now, never mind *do* this now when there's a man lurking around claiming to be my sister's fucking father!"

Gunnar's face was red by the time he finished screaming his question. He slid a hand over his face and let out a long breath.

"That's exactly why we need to discuss this now."

Slayer was serious now, his expression fierce. Hot.

"We don't know how long this fucker has been watching us, but you can bet he knows our whole damn MC." He folded his arms, a slow, smug grin on his face. "But he doesn't know the Lords of Buckthorn."

Wheeler whistled and shook his head. "A brotherhood? Is that what all of this is about?"

He looked at me and then at Slayer, a slow grin forming on his face.

"It might be a good idea. In theory. What do we know about them? No offense."

"None taken." I understood that we both needed to sell each other on this idea, and here I was, the VP, so it was on me.

"We're small, but we do more than all right. The point is that we, both your MC and mine, need bigger numbers sometimes to protect our interests, especially where they might align. Oh fuck."

All of a sudden, I felt like a sword sliced through my stomach, and I sucked in a deep breath.

"Fuck. Sorry." Maybe I should have taken something harder for the pain.

"You okay?" Gunnar's blue eyes examined me with concern instead of suspicion, which meant he was thinking about my idea.

"I'll live as long as I don't get an infection. Not my first gunshot." I flashed a shaky smile, knowing that outside of my own MC, it was important to project as much strength as I could. It was hard at the moment, but I was nothing if not determined.

"We're not trying to share profits or become one big MC or anything like that. Just make it easier for both our clubs to number up when the opportunity presents itself."

It would give us both time to reach our full potential.

"Like shipping your guns with our beef?" Looked like Wheeler had done his homework, at least some of it anyway.

I nodded and arched a brow to let him know I was impressed. "Yep. And we'd hire Gunnar's wife to beef up security at our clubhouse and other businesses."

Gunnar's eyes flashed surprise and then a slow reluctance. "And if you two implode four weeks from now, then what?"

Straight to the point. "Then the only thing that changes is that I won't be fucking Slayer. Business stays the same until you and Curt decide otherwise."

He nodded, satisfied with my answer. It was a test, and I knew it would come; I just hadn't expected it right after being shot.

"All right. We'll give this a shot. You sure this Leon guy is no longer with your MC?"

I nodded. "Positive. Not for more than a year, why?"

"The cops showed up before we...and uh, anyway they asked for the security footage. I told them we had to find the tape or some shit so we could talk to you."

"He's no longer associated or affiliated with me or the Lords of Buckthorn. Period."

Gunnar nodded. "So I'll get them that footage."

I nodded and watched him leave. Wheeler smiled and shook his head before following behind Gunnar, leaving me and Slayer alone. Together.

"So," he said on a sigh.

"So."

"So," Annabelle said, intruding on the almost moment. "I need to examine you now. Slayer can come back later." She gave him a friendly shove towards the door that said she spent a lot of time here and that made me more curious about her.

Chapter Twenty-One

Slayer

"You came back." Chance's voice was full of surprise. I wasn't sure how I felt about it, but the smile she sent my way pushed the rest of it out of my mind.

"I did. Annabelle threatened me, so I decided to wait until she was all the way gone before I came up."

I sent her a lazy smile, and she sat up through a painful looking wince.

"How are you feeling? Really?" I knew it was on the tip of her lips to lie to me, to say everything was fine when her pallid skin told a different story.

Chance opened her lips, now a pale shade of pink, and then snapped them shut as her shoulders relaxed against the wall of pillows behind her.

"Exhausted. In pain. Feels like a bullet tore through my side, otherwise I'm great."

Just those words took a lot of energy out of her, and she sighed again.

"Care to fill in the blanks after I pressed up against you outside The Barn Door?"

My brows dipped low in confusion. "You don't remember?"

Chance pointed to her head. "Head injury, remember?"

I nodded. Like I could fucking forget that I spent the past few hours wishing Leon hadn't killed himself so I could kill the fucker all over again. "You can thank your ex for that bullet Annabelle pulled out of your side."

Her eyes went wide like she really didn't know. "Leon?"

"Yep."

"Shit. Curt's gonna have my ass this time." I could tell the gears were already turning behind those beautiful brown eyes, and I wondered what other burdens she carried.

"At least you can tell him that Leon is no longer a problem."

I figured that news would at least cheer her up so, I let it hang in the air for a moment to see how she really felt about him.

"Once he realized that he shot you instead of me, he was damn near inconsolable."

"Fucking idiot," she grumbled and shook her head. "At least he didn't hit you."

I frowned at her. "It would've been better if he had." Because then the Reckless Bastards would have put him down and gotten rid of the body before the law showed up. I didn't like loose ends, and this all felt like a loose fucking end.

"What else? Tell me."

I nodded and sat down, taking off my boots and laying down beside her. "He tried to get you to leave town with him and once he realized it wasn't gonna happen, he ate a bullet."

There might have been better ways to deliver the news but her reaction was genuine. Her eyes slammed shut and there was real pain in her expression, but on its heels came relief.

"I'm sorry it had to be like that, but Leon made sure that this was the only way it could end."

Her words surprised me. "You really mean that?"

Chance nodded, and her eyes met mine. "I do. He wasn't always like that, and that's what made it so hard. Such a fucking test of my leadership skills, ya know? Remembering the boy and the man he was before he left for the service. He saw shit no man should have to see, before he came back as a new man altogether."

She shook her head at first but ultimately accepted my arms around her shoulders.

"We all come back changed, Chance."

She nodded. "Believe me, I know. But I shouldn't have let the problem get this bad. That bullshit's on me."

"That's a load of shit. The guy was clearly fucked in the head. Nothing you or anyone else could have done would have changed things if he didn't want to be helped."

"You don't know that," she snapped.

She wanted me to be wrong, but I couldn't let her shoulder this when she didn't have to. It wasn't hers to shoulder.

"I do. My best friend, Cal. He was a good fuckin' dude. Always up for a good time and a laugh, always making sure everybody felt included and loved when care packages came in. He was just that kind of guy, you know?"

She nodded, a half smile on her face. "One of the good ones?"

"Exactly. But when we came back, he couldn't handle it. Saw enemies everywhere. He was jumpy as fuck and convinced people were after him. I tried everything I could. So did his wife and his parents. Nothing worked. Six months after we got home, he was dead."

"Wow." Tears streamed down her eyes, but Chance was tough and kept her expression nearly even. "I'm sorry about your friend."

I pressed a kiss to her forehead. "Thanks. Me too. I'm so fucking sorry but that's what helped me realize that some guys...fuck, they just can't handle it."

It wasn't their fault. No one knew how the desert would affect them until they were already there, knee deep in the shit.

"I know, but it didn't have to get this far."

"Maybe. Maybe not. But that's our life, babe. Shit tends to go too far and too often. That's why you proposed this brotherhood, right?"

She nodded with an exhausted smile.

"Of course, it is, but we gotta rethink this brotherhood thing. How about we call it The Counsel? That sounds way scarier than brotherhood. It's got an ominous ring to it, like it's filled with people you don't want to fuck with."

"You make a good point. We're bringing it to an official vote soon. Right now, though, I think you should sleep." Her eyes lowered to slits and she fought it, hard. Not that I blamed her. It was hard to sleep after someone tried to kill you.

She shook her head and tried to sit up but the pain and exhaustion were winning out. "I still gotta call Curt. When are you gonna let me have my phone?"

Annabelle hadn't let her make any calls while she was high on pain killers.

"I'll take care of it. If you trust me with your phone that is?" I quirked an eyebrow and waited for her to answer.

"If they approve The Counsel then I'll be trusting you with more than my phone, won't I?"

I nodded, and she flashed a sleepy grin.

"And here I am, completely at your mercy and in too much pain to do anything sexy about it."

"Gunshot wounds heal," I told her and leaned in, nipping her ear.

Her smile widened, but her eyes stayed closed. "Does that mean you're not here out of some misplaced sense of guilt?"

"Is that what you think?" I wish that was the reason. "I'm here because you took lead in your side. You were out for hours. I wasn't sure if you would make it, so I had to see for myself."

I didn't need to mention that seeing her pass out in my arms had shaved at least a decade off my life.

Chance smiled again, sleepy and sexy as she lifted her arm to hit me. It just barely grazed my thigh. "Asshole."

"Get some sleep. You can verbally abuse me in the morning."

I pressed another kiss, to her cheek, this time as she snuggled close to me on her right side, taking care with her left.

"That sounds perfect, Slayer. Thanks."

She laid her head on my chest with a smile and sleep quickly claimed her.

Chapter Twenty-Two

Ella Mae

"You should take it easy for as long as you need to." Annabelle sat beside me on the sofa in Slayer's living room, where I'd spent the past week recuperating. And...something else.

I snorted. "You mean I still can't ride my bike?"

She sighed. "I mean listen to your body. If you still feel pain when you move, don't move like that." The doctor snapped her lips together in an effort to avoid laughing, but I beat her to it.

"Noted."

"You up for visitors? I ran into some guys on my way in who said they're friends of yours." Based on her smile, I could guess who it was.

I shrugged. "I guess they'll let anyone in here these days."

The door opened and the first thing I heard was Brick's laughter. "You've been here long enough to stink the place up, I see."

His smile was wide and just a little bit relieved.

My own smile was just as wide.

"It's so fucking good to see your big ass, Brick."

The guys had stayed away just in case there was any heat in the aftermath of Leon's suicide. So far it had been routine questions and statements so Curt felt at ease coming by.

"No kidding. You don't look nearly as bad as I was expectin'. I mean you need some makeup but…" he shrugged, easily dodging the pillow I tossed at him.

"Annabelle, this big ugly fucker is Brick, and the guy checking you out is my Prez, Curt."

She laughed, and the sound was as pretty and feminine as she was. I liked Annabelle, but I envied how easily she wore her femininity even as a doctor.

"Nice to meet you both." She turned back to me and pointed a finger my way. "Listen to your body."

Brick snorted. "She don't listen to no*body*, Doc."

"Then I hope you have a nice sedan she can drive." With those words, Annabelle left us alone.

"So how are you? Really?"

I shook my head. "If one more person asks me that I'm gonna scream."

Between Slayer and Annabelle and all the women at the ranch, everyone had given me that sympathetic head tilt while asking that exact question.

"I'm fine. Pain is...manageable."

"And shacking up with lover boy?" Brick arched dark brows my way, his mouth twisted into a teasing grin.

"It's fine, though I was fucking shot so I don't have that post-orgasmic glow you're looking for. Asshole."

Between the pain and the distinct lack of orgasms even after spending the past eight nights in Slayer's arms, I was a grumpy bitch.

Brick and Curt both laughed. Dicks.

Curt said, "The cops came to the clubhouse. Asking questions."

I frowned. "What kind of questions? And what brought them to the Lords' front door?"

He shrugged and took the oversized chair beside the big picture window.

"Leon used to be one of us, and he has plenty of arrests that say as much. They asked basic questions that I thought were fucking odd for a suicide but nothing to jam us up."

The breath Curt let out said he was worried, but this shit show was my own creation so I just nodded.

"They asked about your relationship with Leon," Brick added ominously.

"They did the same to me, trying to find a way to put the blame on me." I felt responsible in a way but damn sure not in a legal way. "Anything else?"

"Hell yeah. The main reason we're in this neck of the woods today."

"Neck of the woods? It's literally the next town over." I rolled my eyes and Curt laughed.

"Anyway, your boyfriend came by late last night with some news."

I stared at Curt blankly. Slayer had come in really late last night, and I was asleep. This morning, well, we had other things on our minds. Things that didn't end in orgasms, but as good as I could get. For now.

"You did a damn good job selling the idea of this little merger. But…The Counsel? Really?"

That teased a laugh from me, and the wince was mild compared to even yesterday. "The Brotherhood was too male-centric considering I'm not a dude. Plus, we sound way more ominous as The Counsel."

Brick snorted. "She's right."

"Anyway, the Reckless Bastards voted last night. The Lords voted this morning, and I cast your vote in favor of joining *The Counsel*." He put his fingers in air quotes and snorted again, in case there was any doubt what he thought of the name.

A satisfied smile crossed my face, and I relaxed against the sofa. "That's good. Did they brief you on the baby daddy situation?"

Curt nodded. "They did. That's fucked up, but we'll do what we can. In the spirit of *brotherhood*."

I rolled my eyes. "Or, you know, *humanity*."

Bricked snorted and shook his head. "Can't believe bikers are fucking selling cattle."

Curt barked out a laugh. "There's a multi-million-dollar sex club on this property, and he's surprised ranchers grow steaks in Texas."

Ah, these bad ass bikers with the hearts of thirteen-year-old boys were my brothers. My boys.

"Brick's special. You know that."

"Special as fuck," he agreed with a crazy-eyed smile.

"Everybody will get a chance to see just how special this weekend because the Lords have been invited to a barbecue on the ranch. A get-to-know-you kind of thing."

"At least the meat will be fresh," Brick grunted, feeling territorial.

"Good. This will be good for the club." I nodded.

"I know," Curt said. "I'm also kinda sorry about Leon."

"I know. Me too."

We all fell silent for a long moment out of respect for who Leon had been to each of us, hell to all of us, at one point in time.

"Let's just hope the next clusterfuck is in the distant future."

Curt let out a bitter laugh and nodded his agreement. It was a constant wish in our circle, but it was just that, a wish.

"Here's to hoping," he said with a grim smile.

"Right," I added.

"We're gonna get going," he said, making for the door. "But all of us will be here Saturday. Wear something pretty."

"You first," I shot back and walked them out, feeling a little sad to see them go, like I should be going with them. But I also wanted to be here. With Slayer.

I hated that it felt so good being here, on the ranch and with Slayer. It felt like a betrayal, of my MC and my heart. This was sex. *Just sex.* It wasn't the beginning of some great love story, I knew that. Sure, he was being kind and attentive right now. But no matter what he said, I knew at least some of it was guilt. And as long as that was true, this could only ever be sex.

Spectacular sex.

And I must've been out of my fucking mind to even *want* anything more than sex after the spectacular shit show that had been Leon. That and the fact that our MC's would now be working together meant this could blow up, too. All roads led to a shit show.

Maybe the universe was trying to tell me something.

"Looks like a whole lot of thinkin' going on over here." Slayer's deep voice pulled me from my thoughts, which must have consumed me because I didn't hear him come in.

He stood there in nothing but a pair of skintight boxer briefs that did wonderful things to the outline of his cock. I unconsciously licked my lips at the sight of him.

"Don't look at me like that."

"Like what?" My eyes grew big and round, as innocent as I could muster.

"Like you wanna eat me up," he growled and the sound was deep and sexy, hitting me right between the thighs.

Oh I wanted to do more than eat him up. "More like lick you *up and down,* but if eating is your thing." I shrugged.

His gaze darkened and his jaw clenched tight. "Dammit, Chance. You're hurt."

I sighed and leaned back against the sofa, my gaze still traipsing over his beautiful body.

"It was a flesh wound that hurt worse than the actual injury, and don't forget, Annabelle already took out the stitches." Earlier today, but still.

Slayer's folded his arms across his chest, and one dark brow arched in a question.

"Okay," I admitted. "It still hurts but only a little. And only when I move."

Slayer's lips twitched as he came closer and sat down beside me, his warm thigh brushing against my own as he leaned in.

"When I fuck you again, Chance, heaven *and* earth are gonna move."

"Tease," I groaned as his lips brushed the side of my neck and slid down to my throat and the tops of my tits. His fingertips scraped along my chilled flesh until he found my warm, wet center and teased the hell out of me. His thumb brushed over my opening until I pulsed. Groaned. The tip of one finger slid inside, and I gasped. Twice.

"Oh fuck. Oh fuck!" I gripped his wrist until he stopped moving so that I could stop moving.

Slayer's deep rumbling laugh pulled me out of the fog of pain, and I looked into his smiling face. "Welcome to blue balls, babe."

I groaned and fell against his chest. "I hate you." I didn't.

"You don't." See? Even Slayer knew the truth. He winked playfully and pulled me closer, taking care to avoid the slightly tender spot where my ex had shot me.

"I totally do," I told him when I felt my body melting into a big damn puddle at that playful wink and sexy smile.

"Prove it." The challenge in his eyes was irresistible, but not so much as those kissable lips. I couldn't help but think about them on my own mouth, or anywhere else on my horny, overheated body.

I was a girl who couldn't resist a challenge, especially a sexy one like this. Wounds be damned when it came to seduction and winning. Right now, both were on the line. I took one hand and slid it slowly down his cheek, his neck, over his shoulder and down his arm until my hand found my own leg and slid upwards.

"Chance," he groaned, but there was no stopping me.

I kept my gaze trained on Slayer because he was better than any clip of porn, hotter than any live sex The Barn Door could offer. As my hand slid into my shorts and panties and between my thighs, there was no better sight than him in nothing but his underwear. My fingers clipped my clit, and my head fell back, and a moan escaped. I slowed my hand to avoid the pain caused by a sharp intake of breath without completely dulling the pleasure. The definition of a slow simmer as my desire slowly increased.

His gaze darkened and intensified as his nostrils flared, and his tongue slicked across his lips. I imagined those lips and that tongue between my legs, tasting and pleasuring me.

"Fuck," he growled, and dropped down on his knees until his lips and tongue *were* pleasing me.

"Oh fuck, yes!" He moved slow and steady until my whole body was covered in sweat, his fingertips pressing into my skin as pleasure lifted me off the sofa. It was the most intense head of my life, because I couldn't get freaky with it. All I could do was grip his gorgeous long hair in my fingers and slowly grind against his tongue.

"Slayer," I moaned when his tongue slipped inside my pussy and licked me. "Fuck!"

His deep laughter sent vibrations through me that only heightened my arousal. My nipples tightened to the point of pain. He pushed my legs farther apart and blew. Then laughed.

"Look at how wet you are. How dripping wet your pussy is."

I smiled. "And it's all for you."

His gaze darkened to black and when his mouth touched me this time, it stayed there until I came so powerfully that I passed out. Completely.

Fuck yeah, it was more than just my greedy pussy in trouble with this long-haired biker.

A lot more.

Chapter Twenty-Three

Slayer

If I was a religious man I'd say that the good weather was a blessing. That some kind of benevolent being was looking out for us, the Reckless Bastards and the Lords of Buckthorns. We gathered on Hardtail Ranch to celebrate the creation of a new and growing alliance. The sun was out, shining like she was showing off, and three little cotton ball clouds hung in the clear blue sky. The smell of charcoal and wood tore through the air along with half a dozen conversations and laughter.

It was a bigger version of our own twisted little family and kind of nice to see. This was one hell of an idea, one that would benefit both clubs and make us all rich men. Something like pride bloomed in my chest at the thought of what Chance, no—*Ella Mae*—had done for all of us.

And Chance was in her element. The past ten days together had been unreal. Unlike anything I'd ever experienced. Sure, there were women when I was on leave, but a day or two in a hotel, not more than a week in my home. And the crazy part was that I liked having her around, liked seeing that sexy little smile she wore that looked like she had a secret. I liked going to sleep with her in arms and waking up with my cock pressed against her soft feminine curves.

It was nice to see the shadows gone from her pretty, brown eyes. It was especially nice to see how easy she was with her guys in her club. It made me realize just how much of herself she held back when she was with me, at least when we weren't consuming each other. Which made it easier to see how familial they were with her. *No jealousy detected.*

Cruz came up beside me and clapped me on the back.

"You gotta be pretty fuckin' flattered we created a whole Counsel just so you could get laid."

He was so pleased with himself; I couldn't help but smile even though I couldn't take my eyes off Chance. She let her hair down, so feminine, blowing in the breeze, a sharp contrast to her black jeans, gray t-shirt, and some weird leather and knit jacket thing she said was more appropriate for a cookout than her beloved leather kutte.

I snorted at Cruz's words.

"That wasn't the reason asshole." I took my eyes off Chance for a second and grinned at him. "But yeah, it feels pretty fucking good."

We shared another laugh and it felt good because shit had been too dark and too serious around here lately. Again.

"It's a fucking good idea."

I had to agree with Cruz. Gunnar was already making plans, and that meant good things for everyone's futures.

"A female VP, huh? You don't like to do shit the easy way do you?"

I frowned at his question. "What do you mean, Cruz?"

He frowned and then once again, Cruz's blue eyes were filled with wicked joy.

"You mean…you don't know? Shit man, wait till I tell Hen about this."

I grabbed his shirt, and the fucker only laughed.

"Don't say shit to anyone about anything." I let him go. "There's nothing to say anything about anyway."

Cruz barked out a laugh and pretended to straighten his t-shirt. "If you say so bro."

He took a long pull from his beer and my gaze instinctively found Chance, laughing it up with Brick like two little kids. "I mean, you fucked someone in another club, even *after* you found out she was in a local club. Both of you know better than that, so y'all came up with this whole Counsel shit so you could be together. Not just fuck buddies. You do realize that, don't you?"

He laughed at my dumbfounded expression.

"Please tell me you realize that, man."

I pushed his hands off me and gave him a dark glare. "You don't know what the fuck you're talking about. You're a married man who sees love everywhere."

He rolled his eyes with a shrug. "Look, this idea is good for both of the clubs, I get all that. But man, this isn't just fucking for either for you. This is real, and judging by that pinched look on your face, you might finally be starting to understand what's going on."

I didn't say anything, I couldn't. It didn't make any sense. "You're talking out of your ass again, Cruz."

WILD

"Believe what you want, but when you need to talk, you know where to find me."

Cruz's gaze landed on his Hennessy, and his smile brightened.

"I'm gonna go promise to use some of that barbecue sauce in the bedroom tonight. You stand over here and keep lyin' to yourself, bro."

"Asshole," I called out as he walked away.

Cruz turned to me with a grin. "I love you, too," he mouthed before flipping me off.

"You two are more like the kind of brothers who grew up together than the kind formed in battle, you realize that?" When I looked at Chance, she smiled up at me.

"Hi."

"Hey, babe. Where'd you come from?"

"Over there." She pointed to Curt chatting with Gunnar and Peaches while Brick was deep in conversation with Holden.

"You were preoccupied with your bromance."

"Bullshit."

She laughed, and the sound was sweet and feminine, reminding me of the way she arched into me and purred when I slid into her.

"Maybe. It's cute but in a totally manly way. I swear."

"You're a bad liar."

"You gonna punish me for it later?" The glimmer in her eyes wasn't lost on me or my cock who stirred to life behind my zipper.

"Maybe. If you ask *real* nicely." The smile the curled her lips at the corners was fucking erotic.

"You want me to beg?"

I shook my head. "Not at all. I don't *want* you to beg, but I'm sure as fuck gonna *make* you beg. Over and over and over again."

"I guess we'll see about that, won't we?"

I leaned in close until her scent wrapped around me, and my lips brushed the edge of her ear.

"I love a challenge, Chance."

Then, because I could, I curled my tongue around her earlobe and sucked until she moaned. Then I took a step back. "Love it."

"You would." She rolled her eyes but her lips were curled into a smile that could only be called affectionate.

Someone lowered the volume on the music, and Gunnar stood beside Curt with his hand in the air, where it stayed until he had everyone's attention. He raised his beer in the air with a wide grin.

He bellowed, "To new friends!"

"To new friends!" everyone shouted back, happy and full and a little bit tipsy.

"He doesn't waste words, does he?" said Chance.

"Unless he's pissed."

That pulled a laugh from Chance, and she leaned in close, heat burning her eyes when she looked up at me.

"Is it late enough to get outta here yet?"

I nodded and clasped her hand to mine. "Yes. Let's go."

It was a ten-minute walk to my place from here, but we could make it in six if we hurried. Five if she let me carry her. I was already moving forward, but Chance's feet were stuck to the ground. I looked back at her, puzzled.

She nodded behind me. "Cops are here."

I turned, and sure as shit, two squad cars pulled up on the dirt path behind Gunnar's house. Two deputies, both of them familiar, stepped out with regretful looks on their faces. My stomach sank.

"Deputies, you here for the barbecue?" Peaches' voice was as smooth as silk and smoky as the best cigar. Her smile had the cops focused squarely on her.

"Afraid not Miss Peaches. Official business." Deputy Kellogg's gaze skipped through the group until he found Gunnar.

"Deputy Byrd will let you know what's going on while I speak with Ella Mae Ambrose."

Chance gasped beside me; her hand gripped mine and fingernails dug into my skin.

"It'll be all right," I whispered, though there was no way in hell it could be all right.

"Don't start lying to me now, Slayer."

"I'll do everything I can to help. No matter what."

Her grip eased. "Thanks."

"Ella Mae Ambrose?" Kellogg looked like he didn't want to be here anymore than we wanted him here.

"Yeah, that's me." Her voice was shaky but still strong.

Kellogg whipped out the cuffs. "Turn around for me, miss. You are under arrest for involuntary manslaughter related to the death of Leon Evans."

"What the fuck," Curt roared into the air. "He fucking killed himself. You do know that, right?"

Gunnar put a hand to his shoulder to stop Curt's tirade.

Kellogg nodded.

"I also know ol' Russ had a heart attack last week, and his deputy has it in mind to make his new job permanent. The dead guy's family is making a stink and here we are."

He cuffed Chance easily and as gently as he could, his sympathy clearly with us on this matter.

"You have the right to remain silent."

Chance's expression never changed. It remained stoic as he led her to the cruiser while she listened to her rights. "I understand."

"I'm glad you do because I sure as shit don't!"

Seeing Kellogg put her in the back of that car with the cage separating her from the deputies tore something apart inside of me.

"Get her a good lawyer, Slayer. Someone who'll take the time to go through everything. Got it?"

I nodded. "Yeah, thanks. Can I have a minute?"

Kellogg nodded. "One minute."

"We'll figure something out. Soon."

Chance nodded. "I know. Just ironic that Leon is still fucking with my life, isn't it?"

"I don't know," I said gently. "Maybe it's because he realized what he missed out on."

Her grin softened, and she shook her head like she didn't believe my words.

"Tell me something, anything else so I can stop thinking about the fact that I'm somehow being charged with Leon's suicide."

I flashed a grin because I knew what I was about to say was reckless.

"Cruz thinks I'm in love with you."

She blinked, expression turned from blank to confusion. "And what do you think?"

Shit, I hadn't expected that question. "I don't know."

Chance flashed a quick, sad smile. "Let me know when you do, because I don't fucking know, either."

Kellogg came then and shut the door, leaving me there as he took my woman away. To jail.

For a bullshit non-crime. "Fuck!"

Cruz's hand landed on my shoulder, and I didn't look at him because I didn't want to see sympathy in his eyes. I didn't want his sympathy. I wanted this shit over and I wanted Chance back in my arms where she belonged.

"We're on it, man."

I knew that. But it didn't make me feel any better about this whole fucking situation.

Chapter Twenty-Four

Ella Mae

It was pretty fucking hard *not* to freak out while I sat in an interrogation box by myself for more than an hour. Possibly two hours. I didn't know because I stopped keeping track at the seventy-five minute mark. But I was doing everything within my power to keep my face blank and my body still as I sat in the hard metal torture device they passed off as a chair.

It was hard not to freak out, even if I knew this was some political bullshit. I heard what that cop told the men. Some fucking lawyer wanted to use my neck to propel him to the next rung in local fucking politics. Too bad for whoever that fucker was. I refused to go down without a fight. And since they had me in a room instead of a cell all this time, I knew it was just a ploy to fuck with me.

That gave their ploy a lot less power.

Still, that didn't mean I was cocky or even confident I could get out of this mess without doing any time. I knew what happened when the deck was stacked against me. Had seen more than a few kids go down for shit they shouldn't have because the system was a train. Once it left the station, its only job was to drop you off at prison. By any means necessary. *Fucking Leon!*

Yeah, it was Leon's fault I was in this mess but it was also my fault. I knew I shouldn't have let it get this far, which made all of this sting a little harder. I couldn't focus on Leon screwing me one last time. I had to figure out a way to get myself out of this mess full fucking stop. If I did time, it would be for my MC or some shit I actually did, not because some guy I used to fuck ate a bullet.

His own goddamn bullet at that.

The door opened, and my gaze went to the man entering the room. I had to hide the shock when I realized it wasn't a detective in a cheap suit. My visitor was a short man with thinning brown hair, shockingly green eyes, and a slightly *more* expensive cheap suit than I was expecting.

It had to be the lawyer, based on the smirk he wore and the overall greasiness that oozed off him. He studied me, and I studied him back, happy to show him that I wasn't afraid of him. Or his threats.

"Ms. Ambrose. I presume you've been mirandized."

I said nothing since neither of those were questions.

"Smart." His grin widened. "But I believe that once you see the stack of evidence against you, you'll change your tune a bit."

I knew that was what he wanted to believe, and he'd work like hell to make sure I believed it before he walked out of this room. But until they tossed me into a prison cell, I wouldn't stop fighting. Hell, probably not even then. I leaned back in the hard metal and tilted my gaze to his.

"And who would you be?"

He blinked, a smartass response poised on the tip of his tongue until the idiot realized he hadn't introduced himself.

"I'm Calvin McAllister, District Attorney."

My lips twitched a little.

"Interim DA from what everyone around here is saying."

McAllister seemed rattled, but he wasn't as new as he looked. Not to mention he was a smallish man who might have thought he had to be tougher just to be taken seriously. Most of all, he knew I was innocent and didn't give a damn.

"For now," he said with what could only be described as an evil smile.

Until he convicted me, then the job would be his.

"Okay, Kevin McAllister, tell me what you have against me."

He held up one small hand with thick fingers, and I swear his grinned widened as he ticked off each item.

"You were at the scene of the crime. You have a connection to the victim. A gun of a similar caliber used is registered to you. He's your ex and from these sworn affidavits, you played with the poor man's head until he didn't know if he was coming or going."

He sat down and leaned back in the chair with the uneven leg. "It couldn't be clearer. I know what happened. You must have pulled the trigger."

A lot of what he said didn't make sense, so I tried to file it away in an organized way to make sure I didn't forget anything for later. Instead of responding and telling him what a fucking liar he was, I stared and stared until he started to squirm.

"You *were* there, weren't you?"

I frowned. "Was I?" From what Slayer and the others had pieced together for me, they'd gotten me back to the house with Annabelle before the cops showed up. But I knew The Barn Door had a shit ton of security, which meant he had to know all of that. Didn't he?

"According to witnesses." His smile tightened, a tell if I ever saw one. Too bad for him I knew the only witnesses besides me and Leon were all Reckless Bastards. A sliver of unease slid down my spine, but I ignored it and kept my expression blank. I had one enemy right now, this dumb fucker.

"This happened at a sex club I believe?" Another smug grin sprinkled with a smarminess he couldn't hide if his life depended on it.

"Why do you believe that?"

He blinked again and stammered over the unexpected question. "*I* ask the questions."

And he'd answered all the questions I had about the reason for my arrest, so there was no point keeping the asshole around any longer.

"You should leave asking questions to the detectives since you didn't ask one."

He opened his mouth to say something, probably something shitty and condescending, but I beat him to the punch.

"I think I'll take this moment to exercise my right to counsel."

That one statement wiped the stupid grin of his bloated fucking face. "Your lawyer? *You* have a lawyer?" His incredulity would have been insulting if I was capable of being insulted by a little boy.

"Am I not entitled to legal representation by law, Mr. *Interim* District Attorney?"

He grumbled under his breath as he stood up, making a big show of going to the super obvious mirror. He tapped on it before he turned back to me, leaning against the mirror with a smile.

"We can make a deal right now and have you back at home in five years. If we have to go to trial, I'll push for fifteen, and I'll get it."

He was bluffing, but dammit, it was hard not to take that kind of bluff seriously. Fifteen years of my life was a long goddamn time. It was my *whole* life really. The time I would decide if I wanted to get married and have kids, maybe take over the Lords when Curt settled down and his old lady made him step down. But fuck, I knew he was bluffing.

"I'll pass on the message. To my attorney."

McAllister smirked. I was sure he imagined I'd make do with some overworked public defender. But I had money put aside. I'd get a shark. Hell, I'd find a fucking mob lawyer if I had to.

The door flew open once again, startling even McAllister. He pressed himself against the mirror as if that made him invisible, but it wasn't a shooter or any other threat. It was a woman in a black suit sculpted to her long, lean frame. The only color was the blood red lipstick and matching stilettos. She wore a predatory expression on her face aimed at the interim DA.

"That's twice my client asked for an attorney, McAllister. I'd hate to bring this to the attention of the Bar."

He heard the threat and hid the fear her words invoked, but not before we both caught it flash across his face.

"Monica Stevenson. You're representing *her*?"

The disdain in his voice didn't bother me. He was the real piece of shit here.

"I am." She flashed a smile that looked more like a grimace. "So I really hope for your sake, that this case isn't as weak as it looks at first glance. If so, what I'll do to you will pale in comparison to the threats you've made."

McAllister snorted, but he didn't say anything in response. I knew then and there; I'd pay whatever it cost to keep Monica Stevenson on my side.

Her blue gaze stared right through him. "We need privacy. You can go now."

McAllister left, and as soon as we were alone, Monica took the seat across from me. I leaned in close and said, "Who are you, how did you get here, and what do I have to do to keep you?"

She gave me a throaty laugh and explained that Gunnar had set up this arrangement. "Don't worry about my fee. We'll work it out. I want to get these scumbags off your back as much as you do. It's personal. Now talk to me. Tell me what happened."

I took a deep breath, in part because the woman was a total badass and I couldn't believe this miracle had dropped into my life. But also, because my side was hurting like a bitch. To take my mind off my pain, I gave Monica a quick rundown of the whole Leon shit show.

"I know they don't have any witness statements," I told her and cast a quick look over my shoulder. I couldn't see anything, but I knew we were being watched. I didn't know if it was *only* the DA who was corrupt.

"Cameras," I mouthed to her along with Slayer's name.

Monica nodded and scribbled something down. "We have privilege so you don't have to worry, Ella Mae."

"Call me Chance," I told her. "It's not you I'm worried about."

She nodded in understanding and flashed a sympathetic smile. "Dr. Annabelle Keyes made a statement and said you didn't do this. Is that true?"

"Yes, it's true." I didn't bother telling her that killing Leon was on my to do list because it didn't seem helpful at the moment.

"All right. And your long-haired friend can tell me everything I need to know?"

I nodded, hoping that was true. Hoping my judgment where Slayer was concerned wasn't as murky as it had been with Leon.

"Yes. But the thing is there's tons of surveillance where this happened and...something doesn't feel right about this. You haven't seen it?"

She ignored my question and said, "McAllister is a piece of shit, and he's not above bending the rules to get his verdict."

Which only confirmed my own suspicions.

"This was suicide, Ms. Stevenson. Leon and I had broken up almost two years ago. He only knew where I was because he'd been following me."

I had a bad feeling about all of this and I couldn't shake it. Had the Reckless Bastards destroyed the footage that could help clear me? Had they done it on purpose?

Being in this cage was already fucking with my head, and it had only been a few hours.

"I'll take care of it. You just try not to freak out."

She explained about the arraignment and bail, which soothed me somehow. Despite looking like a runway model, she knew her shit. She rattled off legal jargon as a reason they had to hold me and generally sounded like she had her shit together.

"It'll be at least twenty-four hours because the judge is off on some fishing trip. As soon as he's back, we'll get you out on bail, and I'll take care of McAllister."

"And what if he's willing to do anything to make sure I'm convicted?"

"He is. But not only do I refuse to lose, I'll die before I ever lose to that sorry ass fucker. Got it?"

I nodded, wishing I could sink into a soft bed and let sleep take over me, to forget about that night. Leon, McAllister. And the pain in my side.

"Good. Now hang in there and don't talk to anyone about your case. Not your boyfriend or your friends, and for damn sure not anyone in lockup. Got it?"

I nodded. "Got it. Tell our mutual friend to get you in touch with my friend Curt. He'll pay your fee."

"Already did. I'll let you know if more is needed." She flashed another of those non-smiling smiles and rose from the chair, which scraped on the cement floor like fingernails on a blackboard.

"Hopefully I'll see you again inside of forty-eight hours. Call if you need anything." Then Monica was gone.

And I was alone. Again.

And surrounded by cops. If I wasn't wide awake, I'd say this was my worst fucking nightmare.

Fucking Leon!

KB WINTERS

Chapter Twenty-Five

Slayer

Being out of the fucking loop was enough to drive me fucking insane, and that was exactly how I felt. A man on the outside slowly losing his goddamn mind.

And it was all Chance's fault.

Okay, maybe *all* was a bit extreme. She couldn't help it that she'd been arrested and charged in the death of her ex-boyfriend. She couldn't help it that the lady-shark lawyer refused to tell me what the fuck was going on even after she asked me ten million questions about Chance and Leon. What she could help was the fact that she'd been locked up for three full days now and had only called me once. Two goddamn days ago.

So like I said, going fucking insane. Maybe I shouldn't be? Maybe I let Cruz get in my head and read too much into this situation. Just because it *felt* intimate didn't *make* it intimate. Right?

Luckily some fuck was pounding on my front door and took my thoughts off the woman who's emotions were as mysterious to me as my own. I grabbed the nearest gun and yanked the door open with a scowl that

I could have saved. It was friendlies on the other side of the door.

"Curt. Brick. What's up? Chance ain't here."

Curt's lips pulled into a lopsided grin. "Aww he's a grumpy ass without his ol' lady."

Brick chuckled. "I heard if you go too long without bustin' a nut, they can explode."

They both laughed, and I flipped them off and stepped back so they could enter.

"What brings the Lords to my door at this ungodly hour?"

It wasn't even ten o'clock in the morning yet, which meant something was up.

"Is Chance all right?"

"She's fine," Curt grunted and wiped his hand on his thigh. "After being sexually molested by the goats on your property, I think you should be more concerned about me."

I laughed and shook my head. "Those girls love bikers, especially the ones who play hard to get."

Those fucking goats were a damn headache, but it was nice to see they weren't just *my* headache.

Curt did all the talking, like any Prez would. "Anyway, we're headed over to spring our girl outta the slammer. Crazy Horse, our Secretary, is already there getting the process started, but we figured you'd want to be there when she comes out."

It was nice that someone thought of me since Chance sure as shit hadn't. And despite that, I was nodding my head like an eager fucking fool.

"Bail? Finally!"

It had been three days when the lawyer said two at the most, but Texans took downtime in general and fishing in particular, extremely seriously.

"Fucking right," Brick grunted and stepped outside to light a cigarette while I locked my door.

"Found Judge Watson *fishing* at his cabin with his thirty-year-old clerk. After a few photos it wasn't too difficult to convince him on the merits of cutting his fishing trip early."

I whistled. "Shit, I'm impressed."

"Good, you should be." Curt's words were bland, plain, but there was a mischief in his eyes as we walked across the pasture to the gravel where we parked the bikes.

The best thing about riding a motorcycle was that I could ride without talking. Without rehashing shit with anyone but myself. I used the short ride to the Opey City Jail to get my feelings in order. Yeah, it pissed me off that Chance hadn't reached out while she was inside, and I tried like hell to suppress the jealousy and anger that she'd called her MC to bail her out instead of me. Especially after what I told her.

Well, after what I'd *almost* told her.

Unlike big city jails, Opey was just another turn of the century brick building like most of the other buildings that lined Main Street, distinguished only by its classic white steeple. We stood in front on the wooden sidewalk and waited as she strolled out. Oversized sunglasses hid her eyes, but nothing could hide the smile on her face.

"Thanks for bailing me out guys."

Curt hugged her first and then Brick before the remaining two members did the same, all smiles and fist bumps for their VP.

"Glad to have you back girl. Get any muff-burgers while you were on the inside?"

Brick's question made her laugh and she smacked his hard midsection. "Wouldn't you like to…know."

Her gaze landed on mine, and I saw surprise there. But also, relief.

"Slayer," Her look of confusion morphed into a smile.

"Surprised?"

"Kind of." She said those two words easily enough, but they were loaded. Luckily, Chance wasn't a woman who spoke in riddles.

"You never came to see me so I didn't figure you'd be here today. But it's good to see you."

Her words came out flat and insincere, and I realized that maybe I was the one who'd fucked up here.

Curt was quick to jump in and fling an arm around Chance.

"Let's make a stop to grab some booze for the party the Reckless Bastards' ol' ladies *aren't* throwin' for ya, then you can go shower and decompress. Yeah?"

Chance smiled and nodded, her expression softening for just a second before it hardened once again.

"That'll be nice."

"Helmet." The word came out of my mouth sharp and harsh as I handed her the helmet, but dammit I was completely out of sorts. She didn't seem happy to see me, and I couldn't fucking figure it out.

"Thanks." Chance hopped on the back of my bike and kept her arms wrapped tight around me as we made the short drive back to Hardtail Ranch.

"You comin' to my place?"

Chance stepped off the bike and glared at me. "Am I still invited?"

I growled, "Get in the damn house," and watched her walk away, up to the front door.

I was being a dick, and I knew it. I'd been in lockup before, and I knew she needed time to herself to shake that shit off, but this felt like it was more than that.

An hour later she finally emerged from the bathroom, a cloud of steam following close behind her, a towel around her and one wrapped around her hair.

"Now I feel almost human again."

Her smile still wasn't full like I was used to. It didn't reach her eyes.

"What the fuck is going on, Chance?"

She froze in the act of drying her hair with the towel and glared at me.

"Care to clarify? I've been in jail for the past three and a half days so I'm not sure what the fuck is going on, Slayer."

The steel in her voice was unmistakable. So was the anger.

"You only called me once."

She huffed out a laugh. "You didn't come to visit at all. That seemed like a pretty big fucking hint dude."

I opened my mouth to tell her she was wrong, that I'd misread the situation, but she kept going.

"You know Annabelle and Peaches came to visit. Gunnar and Cruz too, along with all the Lords. And the Ladies."

Shit. Really?

"But after what I said before…" It was a weak excuse, but I was pissed off too, and I couldn't turn it off that easily.

Chance barked out a laugh and flicked off the towel drying her hair and slammed it down to the floor with so much force her wet hair swirled out like a fan, spraying me with water.

"You said you might feel some kinda way Slayer. What the hell am I supposed to do with that?"

"You didn't say or do anything," I said, the accusation strong in my tone.

"Neither did you!"

Chance got in my face, angry but her voice was low and even, laced with poison.

"You said you didn't know how you felt, and when you didn't show up even once, I figured it out for myself. So exactly what the fuck should I be responding to?"

Her chest heaved, the only sign she was really pissed off. I couldn't help it. I stepped in closer, grabbed the back of her head and crashed my mouth down on hers. It was the only way to still the chaos around us, the only way to stop the fucking yelling and screaming because neither one of us would give an inch. We just weren't built that way. I kissed her long and hard for eternal minutes, savoring the taste of her, the way her body melted into mine. She wanted this, needed it as much as I did and that only made me hotter.

"Chance," I growled as my mouth moved from her lips to the crook of her neck.

The feel of her skin was still slick from the shower under my wandering hands, the heat of my own hands cooling her flesh until she shivered.

"Slayer."

"That's right. Say my name."

The sound that came from her mouth was half laugh and half groan, like she was a little bit amused by me.

"You talk too much," she growled and stopped my next words with a kiss of her own. But this kiss was slow and sweet. It started as an inferno and only grew hotter from there.

Somewhere along the way, she lost her remaining towel, and I lost my control. Hell, maybe I lost my damn mind, too, because I was rough, maybe too rough as I kissed her whole body, and let my beard scrape across her skin, still pink from the shower.

"Slayer," she moaned again. "Please."

That one word, so softly spoken was all it took for the last of my control to snap.

"Fuck me." I stripped my clothes off and stared at Chance as she returned my gaze, so much said between us without uttering one fucking word, exactly the way I preferred to communicate.

"Chance," I whispered back. Her long hair fell around her naked body, giving her the appearance of some kind of fucking nymph, hiding just enough to make me want to see it all.

"Like what you see?" she said with a teasing smile.

"Fuck yeah, I do," I growled. I stepped up to her, slamming my mouth against hers, tasting and devouring her mouth, her flesh until she begged.

"Hurry up!"

Those words brought a smile to my face. I twirled her around, moving that long silky hair to the side so I could kiss down the length of her spine to those little dips right above her ass cheeks. I moved over that sweet little curve and down the backs of her legs until her body physically shook with want. Making my way back up slowly, I gripped her thighs tight and spread them just enough to see the swollen pink flesh, the flash of light as it caught the moisture leaking from her body. I licked that spot and the moan she let out sent a spear of pleasure straight to my cock.

My balls.

"Oh, fuck! Yes!" Her back arched into me as the cries were torn from her lips and her hands fisted the bedsheets. "Yes!"

The woman was insatiable, grabbing a handful of my hair to keep me right where she needed me, where pleasure spilled from her body. The sound of my own carnal moans vibrated against her, pulling more shivers and screams from her body.

"God, Slayer. More, now!"

That was it, I stood to my full height and bent her over, smacked the heart shaped ass even as my mouth watered at the sight of her pussy, pink and swollen from this angle. A low growl emanated from somewhere deep inside me, at least I thought it was me, I couldn't be sure with Chance moaning and begging, squeezing her legs together so her ass moved *just so*.

"You want this?"

"Yeah, I want it," she panted, words breathless and needy.

"I didn't hear you," I told her and let one hand land hard on her ass cheek, turning the skin an angry shade of pink as her lips parted to release a sigh of pleasure.

"Chance," I growled.

"Yes, I fucking want it! I want it, now give it to me, damn you."

My lips pulled together into a tight satisfied smile at her frustrated words. I took a step back, stroking my leaking cock while she squirmed in anticipation. Then Chance, the tease, arched her back to give me a clearer view of that sweet pink cunt.

"It's right...here," I growled and slipped inside her body. It was so fucking wet I could hardly stand it, hotter than fuck and there was no place in the world I would rather be.

"Fuck, Chance." That was just what I did. What she did.

We went at each other like two people possessed, like it had been years since we'd been together instead of just a few days. It was explosive and all consuming, and it scared the ever living shit out of me. Fucking terrified me, actually, but it felt too good to stop. I couldn't let the sounds of those cries of pleasure stop, didn't want them to.

I held Chance tight, held her close as I pounded into her, pulling every ounce of pleasure from her body I could. Gripping her hip with one hand and the back of her neck with the other. I held her tight and pounded into her as she shouted my name. Screamed it at the top of her lungs and then she fell silent.

Several long moments passed where the only sound was my sweat slicked skin smacking against hers, faster and harder until a low groan escaped.

"Holy fucking shii-iiiit!" And then Chance was falling, vibrating and convulsing as her orgasm ripped through her body. She pulsed and clenched around my cock, pulling my own pleasure to the surface.

"Chance," I groaned, at least I think I did. I couldn't be sure when all the blood that should have been in my brain had vacated south and swelled my cock to the point of aching. Only then did she release me, finally milking my body until it was bone dry. Until my legs could barely hold up my weight, and I damn near collapsed right on top of her.

"Fuck, I needed that!"

Second by second her body relaxed into the mattress, the only sign she was still conscious was the way she smiled up at me as she rolled on to her back.

"A lot," she added in a breathy, exhausted moan.

She looked relaxed. A hell of a lot better than she did when she walked out of the jailhouse earlier, and slightly less pissed off than when she stepped from the shower. Good.

"Now that's out of the way, we can talk about the rest of this like rational human beings."

Chance groaned and tried to roll away from me.

"Asshole," she grumbled.

"And don't you forget it babe." I smacked her ass and pulled her body flush against mine, not quite ready to let go of her yet.

Chapter Twenty-Six

Ella Mae

Back to the business at hand. That was where my focus should've been because it was the only damn thing in my life that made sense. Slayer was as much a mystery as he was since the first night in the alley, and I didn't have the energy to figure him out. Why? Oh, because I was standing trial for murder.

Again for the people in the back. Murder. Okay, not *murder-murder* but manslaughter. Either way, they were trying to lock me up for a fucking suicide.

Fucking lawyers. Luckily my lawyer was as good as she was expensive, and Monica was Expensive with a capital 'E'. Curt let me know he'd help out if needed, but even that was tabled for now because we all gathered at the new and improved Lords clubhouse for our first official meeting of The Counsel, name official pending the official vote.

Instead of meeting inside the Lair, we sat around a few tables in Curt's backyard. He had no neighbors and lived on a dead-end street, just in case some shit popped off. And there were no ears to listen.

"All right." Gunnar practically growled as he looked around at each and every one of us. "Since most of the shit on the agenda today is Reckless Bastards shit one way or another, I'll start us off." His gaze slid to Curt, who gave a nod of approval and we got down to business.

"Chance."

It was a strange feeling sitting around a table like this and having guys who weren't Lords staring back at me. Holden's stoic expression was the most calming, but it did fuck all to help in that moment, so I sucked in a deep breath and said what I had to say.

"Monica says the case is weak, but since someone claims they saw me with a blade to his neck in the weeks before his death, it ain't lookin' good."

That day. It was that day that had fucked me, that couldn't be how it all ended. "What are the fucking odds?"

"Wait so you *did* pull a blade on him?"

The surprised, almost indignant question came from Slayer. Surprisingly. Not.

"Yeah, I did. He followed me, again, after I told him not to. And after he backhanded me, if I need another reason."

I hoped Slayer could feel the weight of my glare on the side of his face. Coward wouldn't even look at me.

"We need proof he offed himself," Slayer said.

"The video isn't enough fucking proof? The prick stuck a gun under his chin and pulled the goddamn trigger. Why is this rocket science all of a sudden?" Gunnar smacked the table, nearly toppling the few cans of beer scattered about.

"Apparently not," I said, my attitude coming through in my sniping tone. Something about all of that still didn't add up, and I made a mental note to do more digging when I got home.

"Besides, as far as I can tell it doesn't sound like they have video. McAllister didn't mention it and neither did Monica."

"Why didn't you mention that before now?" Slayer. Again.

"Because I figured the cameras at the club were for show, just like all the bars and liquor stores in town." It was a moot point anyway. "Besides if there was a video, then none of this would be happening, would it?" I huffed.

"Not necessarily," Gunnar said with a sigh. "My old MC went through some shit with crooked politicians. They fight dirtier than the real crooks."

"Seriously guys?" Cruz looked around the room with a playful smile on his face, blue eyes sparkling with unwarranted mischief.

"We're seriously not gonna talk about the fact that Kevin McAllister is prosecuting Slayer's chick?" He looked around again and I had to bite my lips to stop from smiling.

"Home Alone?" When more silence followed, Cruz shrugged. "Sorry but it's funny. Carry on."

Cruz looked so disappointed I flashed him a small smile because I had the same thought during my interrogation. I was about to speak when Gunnar interrupted.

"What the fuck do you mean they don't have video? I handed that shit over myself," he growled, the look on his face brutal.

"McAllister didn't mention it." And I was sure Monica would have if she had it, but she did promise to get her investigator on it. Which was why I'd happily write a big fat check to her law firm. If she'd ever send me the invoice.

"I'll get Peaches to send a copy of the file straight to your lawyer. ASAP." Even as he spoke, Gunnar pulled out his phone and his thumbs flew over the screen.

"Thanks but it won't be enough, not if this crooked prosecutor is trying to use me to launch his political career. I'm headed over to Leon's apartment to see if I can find anything to prove he was a stalking piece of shit so maybe I can stay out of jail."

I knew I sounded like an ungrateful bitch, but Monica's word had stuck with me. She used the phrase *up a creek without a paddle*. McAllister had ambitions and a female biker guilty of murder would be exactly the kind of thing that made a man governor in this state.

"The fuck you are!" Slayer's roar silence all the other chatter in the room, and I shot him a dark look.

"Excuse me?"

"You can *not* go to his apartment." Slayer looked to Curt and then Brick for assistance and then back to me.

"Christ Chance, the last thing you need is for your hair and DNA to be found in an apartment you've never been in, at least I assume that's what you told the detective?"

He was on his feet, glaring down at me like some big bearded Viking with dark hair, concern and anger swimming in his eyes.

"Don't be stupid and get a tampering charge tacked on."

"Don't call me stupid."

"Then don't do something stupid like get acquitted of murder and convicted of tampering. *That* would be dumb as fuck, Chance."

I glared at Slayer, pissed off at him for a variety of reasons, the least of which was for pretending like he gave a damn when it was so clear he didn't. And dummy me, I cared too much. *Another time,* I had to remind myself.

"I need to see if there's any proof he was suicidal or otherwise mentally unstable and that it didn't have jack shit to do with me or the end of our relationship. The only person who knows what to look for is me."

And if I'd done what I should have from the beginning, I wouldn't even be in this goddamn mess.

Slayer nodded, no longer angry but not gloating. Not smug. Contemplative was the best to describe his pinched, almost thoughtful expression aimed at the floor. Then his resolve kicked in, and Slayer circled the table until he was right in front of me, his big hands resting on my shoulders.

"Okay. Then tell me what to look for. Diaries or home movies, computer files, whatever. Tell me, and I'll take one of the Lords with me to scour everything."

I looked up at him wanting to say yes but feeling hesitation vibrating my body.

"Every-fucking-thing," he said, voice deep yet gentle.

It was sweet. Really fucking sweet from a guy who was anything but, and that was exactly why I already cared too much.

"Why? You don't need to get yourself involved in this. None of you do. McAllister will come after you all if he has to."

Curt grunted. "You know we ain't worried about that mother fucker. We're gathering intel," he said vaguely. "Let Slayer go with Brick."

"No. With all the connections to me everyone will be facing tampering charges, or does that not matter anymore?"

Curt glared at me but I saw the way his lips trembled with the force of holding back his laughter. "Slayer and Curt will go to Leon's place to find evidence of his crazy." And that was it, the Prez had spoken. Dammit.

"Curt," I began but Slayer cut me off.

"Getting me involved was your brainchild, sweetheart, so now I'm here and we're all trying to help. All of us."

I sighed and shook my head.

"I can't sit around do fuck all while you guys do my dirty work. I need to do something."

Brick laughed and rubbed a hand over his short hair. "That's what we do, the other Lords' dirty work when he—or she—can't. Me and lover boy have got you covered Chance, don't worry."

At my expression he laughed.

"I mean *worry*. It's fucking prison, but we've got this."

I nodded, agreeing because I had to, not because I wanted to.

"I know he was on drugs but I also think he was selling. Not like dime bags, though. Something bigger. Look for any familiar names written on scraps of paper, scales and packaging. Shit like that." I didn't really know shit about Leon's life, not since we broke up and not since he was booted from the Lords.

"I need something to do."

A rare grin spread across Gunnar's face. "I'm glad to hear you say that because our next order of business is mine. I need an unfamiliar face who can hold her own."

I leaned forward. "I'm listening."

"Perfect. He'll never see you coming."

I didn't know what he was talking about, and I didn't really care, as long as I had something else to focus on while everyone else tried to get me off a murder rap, I wouldn't lose my shit. Not yet, anyway.

The plans were in place at the end of the first official meeting and despite the prison sentence hanging over my head, I thought it went well. If nothing else, bringing these guys together could be my legacy.

Chapter Twenty-Seven

Slayer

"So what do you think of this whole Counsel thing?"

Brick looked at me with a smirk on his face as we climbed the stairs up to Leon's apartment. It was in a decent part of town, not particularly crime ridden but low income and temporary.

"You worried you steppin' on somebody's toes?"

I laughed. "No smartass, I'm just wondering what you think about it?"

"I think The Counsel is a silly fucking name," he said on a sigh. "But it's a good fucking idea for both clubs."

He shook his head like he still couldn't believe me and turned to me when we reached Leon's door.

"Leave it to Chance to make weird shit work."

I didn't know if those words were meant to be comforting or insulting, so I nodded and extended an arm to knock on the door. Not because I expected anyone to answer, I didn't. The police had left the place earlier in the day, even removed all the yellow and black tape. The apartment had been returned to the building manager, who was out of town until the middle of next week.

"No answer."

"Let's hope the place hasn't already been ransacked." Brick gave a short nod and raised his foot to kick the door.

"Hang on, animal." I tried the doorknob and the it swung right open. When I looked back at Brick, he grinned and lifted his wide shoulders and let them fall.

"Discreet is the word of the day."

"So is throat punch," he growled behind me.

I flipped him off, and we shared a laugh, but as soon as we started searching the apartment, silence descended other than a few grunts and one-word commands.

"Kitchen, clear," I said as if we were on a mission.

A pizza box sat on top of the trash and a few beer cans littered the sink, the signs a bachelor lived here. I made my way back through the living room. It was decorated like any other cheap furnished apartment with bland beige sofas and sorta blue carpet. Down the small hallway, I found the bedroom, bathroom and linen closet. All empty and clean aside from the half ass search done by the cops.

"Anything?"

Brick arched a brow at me. "You Bastards really are all former military? Fuckers sound like five-oh."

"Yeah, we really are." I didn't bother to explain that you were never a *former* service member, just active or inactive. "Anything down here?"

"No people if that's what you mean. Let's start looking in the bedroom. Isn't that where little girls keep their diaries?"

He snickered to himself and I joined in, feeling almost like it was me and Cruz taking care of business.

"Should you be saying that when your VP is a girl and all?"

I was busting his balls, and Brick barked out a laugh to let me know he knew it.

"Hell, yeah, Chance ain't no ordinary girl."

Brick turned toward the tall dresser beside the window, and I took the chest of drawers by the door.

"Don't me wrong, she's all woman and all that shit, but she ain't never been no little girl. She tell you about the first time she got shot?"

My stomach churned at the idea of Chance being shot. Again.

"Hell no. I barely survived her most recent gunshot wound."

"Interesting," he said but his smile quickly returned, along with more details.

"The crazy bitch shot herself because the guy was too fucking big and he had the jump on her little ass, holding her from behind with her bent all backward so her legs were flailing around. The rest of us are getting our asses handed to us, no lie. Shot through the side of her leg straight through his thigh. Sent the fucker right to his knees. I knew then and there she was one of us."

The smile on his face, the affection, paid truth to his words.

That was one crazy story. "She wasn't a Lord yet?"

"Nope. Soon after, though."

A comfortable silence settled between us as we got lost in our tasks, combing through Leon's things. It should have been morbid, going through a dead man's possessions, but Leon had been nothing but trouble.

"You not just playing with Chance, are you?"

I glanced over my shoulder to see if he was serious, but Brick was carefully going through every sheet of paper in what seemed to be some sort of writing desk, expression serious.

"Is this where you threaten me if I hurt her?" I asked as I stepped into Leon's bathroom, finding a handful of needles in a small canvas bag taped behind the toilet tank, along with aluminum foil and a glass pipe.

An unopened box of condoms sat beside deodorant and aftershave in the medicine cabinet. The towels and rugs were gone but otherwise the room was empty.

"Do I need to threaten you?"

The idea that he could was laughable. Brick was big and fierce, but he didn't have the training or the discipline I did.

"Chance can take care of herself."

"She *can*," he agreed. "And she will, just like the rest of us. But that don't mean we won't back her up, even if she doesn't know she needs it."

I stepped into the hall and looked at Brick, our gazes connected for a moment of masculine understanding.

"Good to know," I told him.

It was nice to see Chance had the same bond with her club that I had with mine. I never thought much about having a woman in the MC, but it seemed to work for them.

"Chance and I need a moment of fucking peace so we can talk. Figure out what the fuck we are."

The last two nights we'd both been insatiable, out of lust as well as other things. We spent most of last night arguing and fucking. It was hot as hell.

But it was also damned exhausting.

"Good luck," Brick snorted. "I stopped thinking about peace years ago. It's a trap, waiting for shit to cool down before you start living. That perfect time ain't even gonna happen, so take your next moment and instead of fucking, figure your shit out."

Who knew the big man had such insight?

"Yeah, thanks," I told him and returned to the bedroom, making a line straight for the closet.

"This place is a shit hole," he grumbled and lifted the full-size mattress, wincing at the smell emanating from the box spring mattress.

"But shit man…look."

Curiosity piqued, I left the closet to stand beside Brick and looked at the perfect hole cut into the box spring. Two books, one brown leather and the other black. A black duffel bag filled almost to bursting.

"Now aren't you glad I insisted on gloves?"

"Fucking boy scouts," he grumbled and reached for the bag with his gloved hands. "Shit, is that Oxy?"

Odds were good that was exactly what they were. That shit went for a lot of money on the streets because it was addictive as hell, a guaranteed money maker if you were into that sort of thing. As I flipped through the brown leather-bound notebook, I nodded absently at Brick's words.

"Based on the numbers in this ledger, I'd say its Oxy or meth. Maybe that new shit."

"Fentanyl?" Brick whistled and dropped the bag, taking the notebook from my hands. "Shit, who did Leon fuck over?"

"Good question." I opened the black book, hoping it would be the clue we needed to keep Chance around long enough for us to figure our shit out.

"She and Curt are fucking, I know they are even though they both deny it."

"What the fuck?"

I held up the book. "Diary. It's page after page," I told him as I flipped through Leon's drug-addled or maybe mentally ill writings.

"*Why else would he make her VP? Curt is fucking my woman.* All caps and about twenty exclamation points."

"You sure the police went through this place? How could they not flip the mattress? I thought that was police search 101?"

"Fuck if I know," I said. "Your tax dollars at work."

Brick laughed and moved on. "It's funny he picked Curt because they're the closest of all of us, but like brother and sister close. Trust close. Otherwise, she could never be VP."

I knew the dynamics. It's why Gunnar and Wheeler made such a good team.

"Leon was out of his fucking mind."

"*I'll make the bitch pay. She's mine and no one else's.*"

"Crazy bastard. Think that's enough?" I shook my head and Brick nodded his agreement. "You guys really got footage?"

"Hell, yeah. The whole place is wired up, man. Can't have any accusations inside the club."

"Of course. Smart. But you know, that means McAllister is in this shit up to his eyeballs?"

I nodded because, yeah, that thought had crossed my mind a time or two. Or ten.

"Let's hope your intel turns up something useful."

"It will. It's how we got our girl out on bail so quick." In that moment I realized I liked Brick and respected him. He was loyal to his club which said a lot about him, and he didn't mind getting his hands dirty to keep them safe.

"Shit, listen. *I'll kill that long haired motherfucker and then she'll come back to me. She'll have to.* He underlined that shit about fifty times," I said and held up the diary for Brick to see.

"No shit. He was gonna kill you?"

"Seems so. He was a lousy fucking shot, but that's not all. *If she won't leave Texas with me, then we'll leave this world. Together.* It's dated the day he did himself in."

Brick smiled. "That and your surveillance footage should do it. Right?"

"Let's fucking hope so," I told him and tucked the books into the inside panel in my jacket.

"Then you can get some *fucking peace* and tell Chance you love her, right?"

I looked up at him with a frown. "What the fuck is it with bikers and their feelings lately? Is this some new Instagram trend I'm missing out on?"

"What?"

"Nothing. Let's go."

Brick put a hand to my chest to stop me. "We're bikers, we're complicated. And that wasn't an answer."

I sighed but he was right. I did want to have a long talk with Chance about being my girl, but the only way that would happen was if I managed to keep her out of jail.

"When this is over, yeah we'll talk. As soon as I figure out what to say to a woman like Chance."

"Good luck with that," Brick whistled, his smile pure mischief as we made our way out of the front door, shutting it behind us.

"That girl is a terrifying combination of badassery and gentlewoman."

Great. Just what I wanted to hear.

"Let's get this shit to her lawyer right away."

Brick grinned. "Afraid something might happen to one of us?"

"Wouldn't put it past these fuckers, especially since we don't know who the fuck Leon was doing business with."

His expression sobered. "True. We might have enemies we haven't even seen yet. Got anyone else you can trust just in case the right way doesn't work?"

I nodded, appreciating the way Brick's mind worked, thinking he was right earlier when he said Chance's weird idea just might work out.

"I have a person or two," I told him, thinking of all the influential people who came to The Barn Door every week to sate their kinky desires.

Finally, it looked like something close to peace might be on the horizon.

Chapter Twenty-Eight

Ella Mae

When Gunnar said he had something for me to do, I didn't think he meant getting all dolled up to sit in a bar all afternoon. But it wasn't like I had anything better to do and this kind of thing was exactly in keeping with the spirit of The Counsel. Just saying those words made me smile, even if all the guys gave me shit about it. Sure, *the brotherhood* might sound cooler but brotherhoods have been done before. Some might say they were done to death, but The Counsel? That shit is new. *Ish.*

"I'd love to be the reason you smile like that."

I had to stifle my natural tendency to eviscerate any man who would ever try a line like that on me, because right now I looked exactly the kind of woman who would buy that line. By design, thanks to Annabelle and Aspen, who had managed to get me into a short white sundress covered in roses with old lady heels even though Peaches had called them kitten heels. Apparently those chicks knew what they were talking about. Maybe.

I spun on the barstool slowly with an easy smile on my face. "Maybe you can be. What's your name, handsome?"

He smiled, chest puffing out a little at the compliment before he leaned in a little. "The name's Rocco. What's yours?"

Bingo. This was the guy, and yeah he wasn't bad looking, but he looked a lot like Leon had about nine months ago, like he was headed down a bad path. A really bad path.

"Ella."

"Pretty. Is that short for Cinder*ella*?"

Original. *Not.* "Why, are you looking for a princess?"

I let out a bitter laugh that I didn't have to try all that hard to fake.

"Of course, you're down on your luck. It's all I seem to attract these days."

Rocco smacked his lips, a playful smile giving him a more youthful look. "Don't tell me you'd discriminate against a man because life's got him down?"

Oh, he was good. Probably used the same twenty lines on every woman he met.

"Me? Never." I finished off the rest of my watered-down ginger ale and whiskey, knocking it back like a woman who's had a few too many.

"But those types always find better luck and then leave me behind."

Rocco let out a laugh that was deep and masculine. I bet when he was showered and shaved with a haircut, he had his pick of women. Now he looked to be a few weeks away from homelessness, unless of course he had a woman somewhere taking care of him.

"Let me buy you a drink to prove I'm not down on my luck."

I waved to the bartender to bring me another and turned to Rocco, casting a quick glance to the booth by the door where Holden sat with his Stetson on low.

"That's a good start, Rocco."

"It is Ella. It really is." He shook his head and raised his drink when they came. I did the same. "Here's to good luck getting better."

Aaaaand here we go. "Really?"

He nodded, a cat who got the cream smile spreading across his face. "Oh yeah. I got a real big payday comin' up. Real big. Enough for a little vacay for two?"

I giggled and leaned in. "I love vacations. How are we paying for it? Stock wins? Crypto-currency? Coffee beans?"

This was too easy, but I owed Gunnar a thanks because this was fun. "Are you a pimp, Rocco?"

"Nah. I'd get too high on my own supply," he said with a disgusting laugh and no sense of irony. "Can you keep a secret Ella?"

"Totally." I gave an exaggerated nod and leaned in, resting my chin in my hand.

"I got a paternity thing."

I didn't think most people would call trying to take a man's kid a *thing*, but hey, we all had our *things*.

"Wow. Isn't that something guys usually run from?"

When Rocco laughed this time it was bitter, and I leaned against the bar a little more, sensing a long fucking story in my future.

"Nah. There was this woman I used to see from time to time. She was a good lay with a wicked sense of humor. Anyway, she died recently."

According to Gunnar, it had been years, but again, why bother with details?

"I'm sorry for your loss."

"Sure, thanks. So, the last time I saw her she was fat and pregnant, so it's been a while. Then recently my bitch of a wife got it in her head that she wanted better. Can you imagine?"

He shook his head in disgust, shocked by the notion there was better than him, I supposed.

"Hardly," I deadpanned, but he wasn't paying attention.

"Anyway, one night I got to thinking about that kid, and I figured the timing is right. I mean I know she was the kind who got around, but it could work, the kid could be mine."

"And you want a sense of family?"

"Yep," he snorted. "And her guardian now, her *brother*," he rolled his eyes at that for some reason. "He's loaded. Has a big spread with cattle and goats and I'm sure he's got oil. I bet he'd pay a pretty penny to make me go away."

And there it was. Thankfully, Rocco told most of the story to my tits where the tiny microphone was attached to my bra so it should all come through loud and clear for Gunnar.

"What's a lot? Like ten grand? Because no offense Rocco, but I ain't following you out of Texas with a lousy ten g's in your pocket."

"Ten," he scoffed. "It'll be hundred at least, to get me to go away forever."

Oh, this guy was a real piece of shit, and I really hoped he wasn't related to Gunnar's sister.

"You staying somewhere close Rocco?" I leaned in and his gaze fell back to my tits, eyeing them hungrily as he licked his chops.

"Sure am. We can go back to my place. On the highway."

I smiled flirtatiously and ran my fingers through my hair. "Want to get out of here?"

He nodded and finished off his drink. "Where are you holed up?"

"That cute little bed & breakfast run by twins. You know it?"

According to Peaches, the two sisters were the heart and center of the gossip in three counties. Dropping their name would get me access to his shitty hotel room.

Rocco frowned and shook his head. "Fuck that. We can go to my place. I got a fifth of bourbon and clean sheets we can dirty up." He winked, and I had to stifle the urge to vomit.

"Sounds good." I slid from the stool and wobbled a little for show, ignoring the clamminess of his hands working to steady me.

"I've gotcha, Ella," he said, letting his hands do more wandering than steadying.

"Thanks, Rocco. Such a gentleman." I gave his face a little pat and grinned. "I'll follow you. My car is right over there." I pointed to a row of dark sedans.

"You're not fit to drive, babe."

"Maybe not, but I'm also not dumb enough to leave myself stranded at your motel."

His grin widened. "Smart girl. I'll pull around to your car, and you can follow me."

I headed to the little blue box Gunnar had provided and hopped inside. "Did you hear all that?"

"We got it." Curt's voice came through loud and clear. "For a second I wasn't sure if you were buying his shit or not."

"Or not."

"Just checking. We got it all, and we'll be there."

"Good. Gotta go."

Rocco pulled up and ten minutes later we were inside his motel room which smelled like mildew and day-old socks.

"Home sweet home. Make yourself comfortable, Ella."

I flashed another smile and kicked off my shoes. "I think I'll do just that. Thanks, Rocco."

His gaze lingered on my body until I disappeared into the stereotypically disgusting motel bathroom. It was smelly and filthy, but it was better than being out in the room when Gunnar and Curt showed up. A quick look at the clock said it was time, and I reached for the little snub-nosed revolver that was the only thing small enough to fit into this sorry ass excuse for a purse, just in case.

Seconds later, I heard the door kicked in. Rocco let out a very un-masculine scream that made me smile.

"What the fuck?"

The question had more venom in it than I expected, but then silence descended, and I knew he'd set eyes on Gunnar.

WILD

"You're trying to take my kid from me, that's *what the fuck*, Rocco." Gunnar was pissed, and I didn't blame him one bit.

"Sh-sh-she could be mine," he insisted because it was clear his mother hadn't taught him about when to shut the fuck up. A sickening crack sounded and then an anguished cry. "Ow!"

"She is not yours. Do you understand?"

When I opened the door, Gunnar stood over Rocco with a dark scowl on his face, one hand pulled back and ready to strike. Curt stood by the door, letting him know without words that he couldn't leave until they said so.

"I said, do you understand?"

Rocco nodded. "We could take a paternity test," he suggested with a smile that was still on his face when Gunnar's fist slammed down on it.

"Yeah, let's do that."

Gunnar hit him again, anger slowly turning to rage. Finally, Gunnar sat back against the wall.

"As soon as the proof comes in, I'll take that trust fund you got from your wife. And that condo in Miami."

Rocco visibly paled. "Impossible."

"It's called back child support, fucking idiot. See, while you were so fucking worried about getting a big payoff, you failed to realize one important thing. I'd win in any court battle."

"Bullshit," Rocco spat. "A biker who owns a sex club?"

"A military veteran and entrepreneur who hires other military vets. In Texas. Wanna keep this up?"

Rocco shook his head in defeat. "How much are you offering?"

Gunnar barked out a laugh. "Offering? I'm offering to let you live if you get the fuck out of Texas right now and never come back."

Rocco frowned. "But…"

"Never," Gunnar said again, his voice lethally calm. "If I see you again Rocco, I promise that they won't find one piece of you."

Rocco shivered at the threat and nodded his head quickly. Furiously. His gaze slid to me, and he scowled. "You set me up, bitch."

I shrugged. "Damn straight I did, you piece of shit."

WILD

He must've realized there was no winning this game. Rocco gave up. "Fine," he spat out. "I'm gone. Whatever."

"I'll be back tomorrow at ten in the morning. You'd better be history." Without any further threats, Gunnar stood and left the motel room, me and Curt on his heels.

"You look weird dressed like this," Curt said with a frown. "Too girly. It's weird."

"Thanks, fucker." I smacked his arm.

"You did good," Gunnar said, his words genuine even as anger lingered in his expression. "Thanks."

"Anytime. Playing dress up is fun."

It had been exciting too, but now I was exhausted. And yeah, I was eager to get back to Slayer.

Chapter Twenty-Nine

Slayer

Chance was so lost in her thoughts, her troubles that she hadn't heard the bathroom door open. It had a loud as fuck squeak I'd been meaning to fix for weeks. Okay, months. So, I wondered what was on her mind.

Was it Leon? Or was it all the shit he'd laid at her feet since he got mixed up in whatever shit me and Brick had found earlier? I didn't know what was on her mind, and it wasn't usually my style to ask, but maybe Chance and Brick had a point.

Maybe this was exactly what it felt like. Something *more*.

More than what, I had no fucking clue. Chance was clearly more than a piece of ass because we'd damn near been living together for the past few weeks. And it was more than casual dating, since we created a whole fucking alliance just to be together.

Shit. We did all this to be together. How the fuck did I not realize it before now?

And there was Chance on the other side of that shower door, nothing but a silhouette with the weight of the world on her shoulders. And here I was on this side, wanting nothing more than to relieve her burden. So, I did, taking less than two seconds to get rid of my clothes and slip in behind her, wrapping my arms around her shower-slicked skin and pulling her close to me. "Long day?"

She nodded wordlessly and leaned back, letting me take some of her burden, even if it was only physically.

"Wanna talk about it?"

Chance shook her head against my shoulder, and a feeling of warmth washed through me. She was exhausted and a little vulnerable, and goddammit that got to me in a really big way.

"Good. Talking is overrated." It would have been easy to take what I wanted with her naked and wet, but I couldn't. Not now.

Instead, I took a step back so my cock wouldn't brush right up against her ass. I put my hands on her shoulders, digging my fingers deep into the tense muscles until she relented. Moaned. Dropped her head forward.

"Slayer."

"See, Chance, there are all kinds of ways I can get you to moan my name." I whispered the words in her ear, that little catch of breath doing nothing to keep my arousal at bay.

She let out a small laugh, the tension leaving her body with every press of my fingertips.

"Is that so?"

"Mmm-hmm." My hands moved from her shoulders to the muscles that went down the length of her spine, pulling out erotic groan after erotic groan until her voice broke the silence.

"Stop. Teasing."

"Who's teasing? I'm just comforting you."

"Ah," she moaned and tossed her head back against my shoulder. "Is that what this is, comfort?"

"Yep."

She gasped at the popping sound at the end of the word and took a step back until we were skin to skin again.

"Are you not comforted?" I moved my hands from her shoulders to her hips, pressing my lips to her spine and kissing a path all the way down to the curve of her ass.

"So. Comforted," she panted when I spread her ass apart and found that dark tight spot most women feared.

"Yes, Slayer!"

Not Chance. Not my girl. She rested her palms flat on the shower wall, bracing her arms and legs as my mouth licked her between her legs until she was a writhing, crying mess in my arms. I licked and licked, gripping the back of her thighs to keep her standing, to keep her right where I wanted her while my tongue teased and tortured her, prolonged her pleasure until she begged.

"I need to come, Slayer."

I flicked a tongue against her clit and looked at her, pink and swollen and pulsing with need. With the heat of desire and the urge to come. "Not. Yet."

"Please." My cock leaked at that one word, spilling from her lips like a prayer. "Slayer."

"Please?" I pulled her clit between my teeth, nibbling it gently, which only heightened her pleasure, pulling out loud wailing cries from her throat. Then I slid my middle finger between those beautiful ass cheeks and deep inside until she moaned, "Yes!"

She bucked back against me and then forward to get to my tongue, riding my face like we both wanted.

"Slayer, yes!" she wailed, "Oh fuck!" signaling to me she was there.

I held Chance as she rode herself to orgasm, to the kind of pleasure that was so all-consuming it required every ounce of energy to ride it out. The moment her orgasm ended, her legs gave out.

"Just can't get enough of me, huh?" as she fell into my arms.

Another laugh escaped, and she tried to find my face under the shower spray, making visibility limited.

"I feel too good to give you shit for that ego right now."

"I'll take it."

Chance laughed again, and I knew I was beyond in trouble. I was so thick into trouble that I feared I might end up like the rest of my MC, in love.

"I guess I should get up," she said with a laugh. "But I don't want to."

I squirmed, because even though I loved the feel of her naked body on top of mine, the bathtub was hard as fuck.

"You stay here and I'll get up."

She squirmed and laughed, but that laugh quickly turned to a shriek when the water turned cold.

"Holy fuck! Holy fuck! Holy fuck!" I could honestly say I'd never seen anyone move that fast. "Holy shit that's cold!"

"Got you out, didn't it?"

She glared at me, at my smiling face and then at the shower, her glare intensifying.

"You didn't."

"I might have."

"Asshole," she accused.

I shrugged. "Maybe."

That anger turned quickly back to lust as she took in my naked body, my cock hard and jutting out almost like he was reaching for her.

"Asshole."

"You already said that."

"It's true twice." Her lips twitched and she turned and walked out of the bathroom, unaware of how fucking sexy she was when she was all riled up.

"Yeah? What are you gonna do about it?"

She whirled on me and pushed at my chest, growling her frustration when I didn't budge. Chance was angry and afraid, and I didn't blame her. She was also spoiling for a fight.

"Fuck!"

"That sounds like a better idea than fighting." I grabbed her wrists behind her back and held her close to me, smiling at the way her nipples beaded instantly.

"I don't want to fight. Or fuck."

"Bullshit. You want to do both. Why?"

Brick's earlier words came back to me then, *a terrifying combination of badassery and gentlewoman.*

"Shut up," she insisted, angry like a cornered animal, and I understood.

Chance was scared.

"Welcome to the fucking club, sweetheart." She looked at me in confusion, and I took advantage of the moment of quiet and pressed our lips together, held her tight as we fell, still wet, to the bed.

She didn't fight me at all. She melted into me, returning my kiss with enough fire to fuel a million jets. My heart smacked against my chest with every swipe of her tongue, every time her hands slid across my skin. Whatever was bothering her, it wasn't this.

It wasn't sex.

It was us.

Then, like a woman possessed, Chance pushed me away and dropped to her knees, looking up at me as my cock slowly disappeared down her throat. Her gaze never looked away as she took me deeper and deeper, licking my sac every once in a while, just to make sure she had my attention.

She damn well did.

"Stop!"

It was too much but that wasn't it.

"Fuck, I love the feel of your mouth on my cock." But it wasn't what I wanted. I mean, *it was*, but it wasn't. It didn't feel right. It felt like she was hiding.

"Then why am I stopping?" Her tongue flicked out and captured the drop of pre-come on my cock and she moaned. "Why, Slayer?"

Fuck she was a tease and a half, and when she took my cock again, I was powerless to push her away again. So I held her close, cradled her face so she couldn't look away, couldn't hide. I stared into those honey-brown eyes while she ate my cock, sucked me long and slow and hard until my spine cracked and a sheen of sweat covered my body.

Chance wanted to look away, but I held her there, watching the play of emotions she tried to hide. From me or herself, I didn't know, but suddenly I was eager to know what those feelings were.

"Mmm," she moaned and closed her eyes for several long seconds, giving her a serene look that caught my breath. Literally.

"Chance!" Her eyes flew open, and what I saw there flayed me open. It was more than lust and affection, but those were there too. I couldn't quite figure out what it was, but I had a pretty damn good idea. And it was scary as fuck.

Suddenly I had to have her. I needed her. Right. Fucking now. I took a step back and she stood, her gaze wary but intense. Then Chance pushed at my chest, again and again, until my legs hit the bed. She smiled and pushed me onto my back as she climbed on top of me.

"Slayer," she moaned and tossed her head back, hips grinding so her wet pussy slid up and down the length of my cock.

"Yes!"

It was an erotic image she made, using my body to please herself. But she was hiding. Again.

"I'm waiting Chance."

One brow arched in my direction, and I sent the same expression back. "Feeling a little dissatisfied?"

"Feeling like I need to be deep inside you," I growled.

In response, Chance smiled. She leaned low until her tongue found the spot just above my belly button, and she licked a trail of heat up the center of my body. She didn't stop until her lips were on mine, her tongue danced with mine to a tune I'd never heard. But somehow knew all the lyrics and dance steps to it, as if I'd heard it in a dream. At some point she pulled back with a growl, hips still moving in a slow, dragging slide.

"You should go with that feeling," she whispered and gripped my cock.

Slid slowly down the length until I was buried deep.

"Oh, fuck, Slayer. Yes!" She was magnificent with her head tossed back in pleasure; her hands firmly planted on my chest as she rode us both. She rode hard and fast, a woman running away from her demons, her feelings, and right towards ecstasy.

"Slayer!"

"Yes, Chance. Let go."

She was close, I could feel it in the way every inch of her vibrated. The way pleasure emanated from her, and the way she clenched around my cock, greedy like she couldn't get enough.

She rode harder and faster, chasing down her pleasure until she found it.

"Oh! Fuck! Slayer." The last word fell from her lips on a small cry as her arms trembled. I gripped her hips and pumped up into her.

Chance held on and bounced around, crying as she was overwhelmed with physical pleasure. Erotic satisfaction. It was a sight to behold, and I thrust up into her, hard and fast. A nipple within tasting distance bounced into view and I pulled it into my mouth. I sucked and fucked until she yanked every drop of satisfaction from me that she could.

"Chance!" That was it. One word. Her name spilled from my lips over and over and if I didn't feel so good, I might have been embarrassed.

But I wasn't.

I was happy. Satisfied.

Ready to go again.

Chapter Thirty

Ella Mae

"I'm going to keep it real with you, Ella Mae." Monica's voice through my phone was as no nonsense as ever, but the worry she projected triggered my own.

"Something fucky is going on over at the DA's office. I'm looking into it, but in the meantime, don't talk to anyone. No cops and definitely no fucking lawyers. Period. Got it?"

I nodded, even though she couldn't see me, and blew out a long breath as my legs gave out and sent me falling on to Slayer's sofa. Slayer's because I still hadn't been home. Didn't want to go there, not now anyway. Couldn't even think about going there and seeing Leon's face on every photo, every gift he'd ever given me. Shit, I was afraid everything would remind me of the fucker.

"Yeah, I got it Monica. Thanks."

"Buck up. This is the kind of fuckery that usually ends up with charges being dropped. If you don't hear from me, I'll see you Tuesday at the courthouse. Right?"

I nodded again. "It's not like I have anything better to do."

"It's just a preliminary hearing, but you need to be there. Dress like you're going to a job interview and hide those tats, yeah?"

"Yeah, I will." I sighed. Why were people still so judgmental about tats? Everybody had them.

"Great. I'll be in touch, but call me if you have any questions, concerns, or fears." She sounded so in control.

"Other than spending my life behind bars?"

"Yeah," she laughed. "Other than that. Because you won't be spending your life behind bars. I'm going to get you cleared of all of this."

"Okay. If I think of anything, I'll call."

"Your boyfriend did a good job in hiring me, Ella. Worry if you must, but I'm damn good at what I do."

That was little comfort to me and all the men and women sitting in prison around the country for crimes they didn't commit. "Right. Thanks." I said and pushed the end button. I had to trust she knew what she was doing.

A knock sounded on the front door, and I panicked. My hand automatically went to my gun and

I groaned, wondering when the hell Leon's stalking would vanish from my memory. Life was stressful enough to jump every time someone showed up at my front door.

Well, *Slayer's* front door.

My legs felt heavy and wooden after my conversation with Monica, but somehow, I made my way to the door and pulled it open. Peaches stood there with Stone in her arms, Annabelle beside her with a hand wrapped around Maisie's. Hazel, Aspen, and Hennessy surrounded her, looking like some kind of gang. Why wasn't I relieved?

"Hey girls. What's up?"

"What's up is we're having a party tonight. Everyone is coming."

Peaches' words were matter of fact but there was a hint of a smile that played around her lush mouth. "Everyone."

I wasn't in the mood for a party, and I wasn't equipped to deal with a gaggle of determined women. *Girly* women.

"Uhm, I'm not in a party kind of mood."

Peaches flashed a grin at Annabelle. "Told you she'd say that."

"Look," Aspen said, trying to be the voice of reason in pigtails and a rounded belly. "We know things have been shitty lately and that you're probably scared. Really scared," she added with a shiver. "But tonight is important, more for you than the rest of us. We're just wives. Girlfriends. But, you're one of them."

I frowned, confused. "What are you talking about?"

Peaches rolled her eyes and shook her head.

"Slayer didn't tell you?"

Slayer hadn't told me much of anything for the last few days, and I was damned confused and on the verge of packing up my shit and returning to my own damn place.

"Tell me what?"

She sighed. "Ford is getting patched tonight, maybe right now. The guys are at the clubhouse doing whatever they do and when they come out, we're partying. All of us. You included."

I wanted to tell Peaches she wasn't the boss of me, but I wasn't fully convinced she wasn't the boss of everyone. "Fine. What time?"

"Oh, I don't think so sister." Hazel stepped forward and grabbed my arm. "We're all going to the big house to get ready together. It's a girl thing, and you're included in that."

"I'm not...I don't..." Shit, I had nothing. I spent time with the Ladies of Buckthorn sometimes, but the fact was I wasn't one of them, and I never would be. I wasn't an old lady, a side piece, or a fuck hole. I was a patched member, but with these women it could be different, maybe I could be different. Still me but maybe the more girly parts of me.

"Aww, I think we broke her," Hennessy said with a sassy smile.

"I don't have anything to wear, and I'm not good with...girl stuff."

Peaches barked out a laugh. "None of us are. It's fun and chaotic, but it's ours. Come on."

I knew when I was beat. I was a badass biker chick. A killer in tight blue jeans. It didn't happen often, but this was one of those times, I wanted to be a part of. I nodded and took a step back so they could enter if they wanted. "I need to grab some things, I guess."

"Your regular badass biker babe look will be fine," Aspen said with a wistful look. "I wish I could pull it off."

Peaches laughed. "And we all wish we could pull off the prom queen, but we can't."

"That's right," Annabelle said with a grin. "We all have something we wish we had. Big deal. I'm a nerdy ass doctor who wears glasses and cardigans, but I'm still in love with a biker."

"I'm a covert hacker chick and a mom and I'm in love with a grouchy biker," Peaches said with a grin.

Aspen opened her mouth, and I held up a hand. "Don't you dare. Okay you're all in love with bikers, big deal."

"So are you," Annabelle offered.

"No, I'm not." I huffed.

After a beat of silence, they all started laughing. "Oh shit, she's worse off than we thought," Hazel said with an amused grin.

"I'm fine. There's no reason to worry about me," I insisted, feeling cornered.

"Chance, you're practically living with Slayer, and I'm pretty sure you guys are sexing it up day and night," Peaches said with a salacious eyebrow wiggle.

"You united both of the MC's just to be together, so please, stop fighting it, sister. Tonight is the night to get your man. Claim him. Make him yours."

WILD

That had been my plan. Well *that* or pack up and go home. I was still undecided.

"If you don't," Hennessy said with a teasing grin, "I'm sure those Buckthorn ladies will happily swing from his vine for the night."

At the stunned silence, she looked around with a frown. "What? It's 'cause he has that whole Tarzan thing going on."

Slayer was more Drogo than Tarzan, but she made a good point about the Ladies of Buckthorn. One look and they'd be killing each other to get up close and personal with the charming biker. *My* charming biker.

"Oh, hell no! I don't think so."

"Whoa," Annabelle said with a laugh. She clapped her hands like she was ready for business.

"Well, look who finally showed up," Peaches said with a smug grin. "Can we go now before this one wakes up from his nap?"

Like some kind of modern day tribe, half a dozen women and a few kids marched across Hardtail Ranch and prepared for one of the most important rites of passage for any MC. Becoming a patched member.

Over cocktails and makeup tips, I thought about what the girls said. I listened closely to what my own heart had been telling me for weeks. It had chosen, and it wanted Slayer. Hell, I wanted him, too, but was it too soon?

Was it even a good idea now that our clubs were officially in business together? Was I brave enough to go after this? To reach out and grab it without letting thoughts of Leon taint every moment we spent together? I saw Slayer's doubts, even though he tried to hide them. I knew those doubts kept a barrier between us.

As I slipped into my favorite pair of black jeans and slicked on a borrowed hot pink lipstick, my resolve strengthened. I was a badass bitch who went after what she wanted, whether that meant becoming the first female VP of a MC in the state of Texas, learning to ride a bike, or claiming a biker for my own, I made shit happen. And that's what I had to do, or risk losing Slayer forever and watching him move on with someone else.

That thought made me physically ill, which meant there was only one thing left to do.

Claim my man.

Chapter Thirty-One

Slayer

This shit right here. Brotherhood. Friendship. Fuckery. This is why we walked straight into hell each and every time one of us was in trouble. We bitched about it, gave each other shit about it, but at the end of the day we were here. Because of this.

Gunnar stood in the Sin Room at the head of the table with a wide grin on his face and a big ass drink in his hand.

"Raise your glasses for the newest member of the Reckless Bastards, Opey Texas Chapter." We all raised our glasses with a smile for the rosy-cheeked kid with a chest as broad as linebacker.

"To Ford."

"To Ford," we all echoed.

Gunnar clapped him on the back and squeezed his shoulder.

"Welcome to a lifelong brotherhood, kid. You've proven to be one hell of an asset the past few years. Should have done this a long time ago." He ran a hand through his newly cropped hair and blew out a breath.

"Anyway, shit. Ford you've proven time and again that you're one of us. A true brother. And this," he held up a brand new leather *kutte* with brand new patches, "makes it official."

"Put that shit on, pretty boy!" Cruz released a loud whistle and clapped even louder until we all joined in.

It was nice to have something good to celebrate. And it was damn nice that it wasn't something like the birth of another damn kid. Not that I had anything against kids. I didn't. But it was nice to know that tonight would be an adult only kind of party with booze and weed instead of cake and ice cream. Ford was a good kid, and I was happy now to call him brother.

"Thanks y'all," he said, still sounding every inch the farm boy he'd been before Uncle Sam molded him into a warrior.

"This is unbelievable. I'm humbled. And excited to no longer be a prospect." He cut a look at Gunnar that made us all laugh.

"Yeah, yeah. All right fuckers, let's drink to the kid and get on with the celebration!"

Cruz caught up to Ford first. He belted out a laugh and flung an arm over his shoulder.

"Now that we're all wifed up around here, you get dibs on all the hot bitches hangin' around. And since I'm out of the game, your odds have just gone up."

Ford laughed. "With this face I'll have to use a bat to keep them away."

"It's a good thing our girl Chance has Slayer all twisted up, otherwise you'd have to battle the great pussy *slayer* just to get it wet," Wheeler said with a laugh and a clap on the back. "Now it's just you and Mitch, and he's a professional head shrinker, so he's got you there."

Ford laughed again, his skin flushed pink with happiness. Pure joy at finally reaching the end of a long damn line. "I ain't scared."

"Exactly right, my man. Don't be scared. You're a goddamn Reckless Bastard now," Cruz said before leading the parade from the basement of The Barn Door all the way back to the patch of green behind the big house.

"Damn, you girls have outdone yourselves. Again." Holden's deep voice was about the only damn thing loud enough to cover the music and the laughing women.

"Looks and smells fantastic."

He wasn't wrong. I didn't know how long we were in the Sin Room, but the women had managed to turn the backyard into a fucking wonderland with twinkling lights, plenty of food, drinks, and music.

Aspen was on her feet first, belly slightly swollen with baby number two as she wrapped her arms around Holden. "We got some brisket tacos, just how you like 'em."

"Sweet and spicy, just like my girl." He pulled her in close and dropped a kiss on the top of her head that started an ache deep in my chest.

"And you invited everyone," Gunnar said with a smile, flashing a nod to Curt. He stood with Brick and a couple of girls near the tables loaded up with food and booze.

"Welcome Lords of Buckthorn. And Ladies," he offered with a charming smile that seemed to warm them right up.

"Thanks for having us. All of us," Curt said, raising his own drink high in the air. "Welcome to life in the MC kid!"

"Thanks," Ford said, his gaze already sizing up the half dozen or so Ladies of Buckthorn mingling with the girls.

"And welcome to The Counsel," Brick added with an eyeroll. "Name obviously pending."

That pulled a laugh out of everyone, but I was hardly paying attention. Seeing Curt and Brick meant there was a good shot Chance was here.

I scanned the crowd until I found that long, dark brown hair failing down her back. shielding her Lords of Buckthorn patches from view. Couldn't fool me, though. The red and white threads gave her away. *Chance.* She was here. Alone and off to the side, observing but not really interacting with anyone. An island.

A beautiful fucking island if I ever saw one. She turned so I could see her. All of her, and my breath caught. Damn, she was beautiful, and today she wasn't even trying. Honey-brown eyes lined with black, giving them an eerie glow, but her lips were bare, and her skin was smooth. Clean. Her expression didn't belong at a party or a celebration; it was vacant and forlorn.

It was time. My legs carried me across the grass, my heart racing with every step I took, because I knew with the same certainty I felt joining the Marine Corps. Joining this MC. I loved Chance.

Goddammit, I was in love with her, and it scared the shit out of me.

I had to tell her.

Now.

"Hey." I stopped in front of her, well *behind* her since she was scanning the tables once again.

"Looking for someone in particular?"

Chance turned her sad eyes my way and gave me a half smile.

"Hey you. Nope, just…looking."

More like avoiding, but I didn't say that.

"How about a tequila and lime to warm you up?" I offered, hoping she'd loosen up.

"Already had one. Thanks."

Okay. Was that a brush-off?

"Are you all right? I mean, I know that's a dumb fucking question with everything hanging over your head right now, but are you?"

Shit, I was fucking this up and Chance was looking at me like I was an idiot.

"I'm as okay as I can be, considering. How are you?"

"Worried about my girl." Because no matter what the hell we both were trying to tell ourselves about this being just about sex and gettin' off, we were both full of shit. She was mine and I was hers. Period.

"Is that what I am, Slayer?"

"Fuck yeah. Unless you don't want to be?"

Holy shit. How had that not occurred to me? Chance was a woman, but she wasn't a typical woman. Hell, maybe she didn't want a relationship, and especially not after all the shit Leon put her through.

When she took her time answering, I started to worry. When her gaze shifted down, my stomach dropped.

"Of course I *want* to be."

I could hear the 'but,' even though she didn't say it, and I couldn't bear it. What if she didn't want me?

My lips started moving and words spilled out faster than I could regulate them.

"I love you Chance. Hell, I don't even know when it happened. It probably took me too fucking long to even realize what the feeling was, but I did figure it out, and I'm here now, telling you. I'm in love with you."

Her smile was kind of snarky. It was a familiar look on her, but I realized she looked uncomfortable.

"I love you, too, Slayer. It's all fucked up, but I do."

The words came out barely above a whisper, and they didn't fill me with hope or happiness or anything.

"Are you sure? Because it doesn't sound like it."

That teased a reluctant smile from her.

"Fuck you, Slayer, I know I love you. I can't even believe it, meeting you while Leon was making my life a living hell. The hot fuck in the alley doesn't do anything for my reputation, but I fucking love you. And here you are, big and sexy and charming as fuck. And I fell. Hard."

That sounded good, too, and I realized that maybe I'd spent too much time just banging women because I could. Arms folded, I looked her in the eyes.

"I love to hear those words, Chance, but I feel a big fat 'but' coming."

Her smile held no amusement, and when she nodded, my whole heart stopped. One beat, another, and then a flutter while I waited.

"But we can't be together. Not now, anyway."

"Bullshit!"

The word came out easily. Automatically, and Chance reared back as if I'd hit her.

"Okay." That was it, one word. One fucking word, and she wrapped her arms around herself, deflated and on the verge of tears. Like a beaten woman.

"That's it? Okay? Are you even for real right now, Chance?"

It didn't seem like just a few seconds ago I was professing my love for a woman I currently wanted to strangle.

"Why, Chance? Why can't we be together? Because you still love Leon?"

"You know I don't."

"Do I?" I'd had my suspicions for a while now, and with his funeral scheduled for the day after tomorrow, those doubts crept back in.

"Right. Well, then *that's* why we can't be together." She let out a bitter laugh and swiped at a tear that slid down her cheek.

"Stupid me, I thought it was because I might spend a good chunk of my life in prison, and *that's* why we shouldn't be together. Turns out you don't even fuckin' trust me."

She turned and walked away. A feat that was made difficult from the soft ground that had grown softer with the wetter than average weather.

I grabbed her arm before she could get too far away.

"Don't walk away from me, Chance."

She yanked away from my grasp with fire in her eyes.

"Don't put this on me, Slayer. I love you, and I want to be with you, but I won't ask you to wait for me."

"That's the point, Chance, you didn't ask. I'm telling you I want to be with you, just you and you're telling me why we can't. I know what happened Chance, I was there. I know what's at stake, and I don't give a damn. It's too bad you don't feel the same."

If she could walk away from us so easily, so could I.

Chapter Thirty-Two

Ella Mae

After spending so much time at Slayer's place on Hardtail Ranch, I felt like a visitor in my own home. My own damn home, and now I felt like I didn't belong here, and it was all because of a man. Again.

Apparently getting shot by my ex wasn't enough of a lesson, because I'd already fallen in love *and* gotten my heart broken again. By a different man completely! Talk about a dumbass. I guess I was one of those people who never learned the lesson no matter how many times I'd repeat it. Falling for Slayer was beyond stupid. Beyond idiotic when you think about the fact that our MCs are now connected and will be for the foreseeable future.

Typical Chance. Do things first and *then* think about the consequences later.

No, that wasn't true. I walked around my apartment in my fuzzy slippers, shaking my head. I spent my time cleaning and getting things in order, just in case these were my last few days of freedom. I might have jumped Slayer's bones before I realized he was in another club, but that was my only mistake.

I did the right thing at Ford's patch party. I knew it, and in time Slayer would know it too. There was no fucking way in hell I'd let him waste his life waiting for me while I rotted in prison for who knew how long. That was some shit I'd never be down for.

Ever.

It just sucked that he couldn't see it too. That we wouldn't spend these last however many days we had together enjoying each other. Being together. Loving each other.

Instead, I slept in my own bed last night, all alone, and spent most of the day trying to get my affairs in order as much as I could. Should I get the utilities preemptively turned off or wait until a guilty verdict came down? I had no idea, but every thought about every little thing just made the burden seem heavier.

Harder to bear.

But it had to be done. With me locked up, Curt would need someone to act as number two, which meant I couldn't put the burden of maintaining my property on him. Or any of the guys. "Now I need to think about selling," I growled and went to the fridge, yanking a brown ale and slamming the door harder than I needed to just because it made me feel better.

I'd barely gotten one good sip in when a knock sounded at the door. It was too early for any of the guys to show up since I was pretty sure they'd all be sleeping until the sun set on today. I'd acted as the designated driver last night, and though a few of the guys crashed at the mostly empty bunkhouse on the ranch, most made their way home with me around three in the morning. So who was it?

I had an insane thought that it might be Leon, but that was ridiculous, and I laughed at myself just for thinking about him. Then, another thought occurred. It might not be Leon, but it could be an angry family member out for revenge. Shit. I reached for the gun I kept under the front table and looked through the peephole.

"Shit Peaches, you scared the hell out of me."

I opened the door to her smiling face.

"Damn, girl. If knocking makes you that jumpy, I'm not sure you're cut out for prison."

I snorted and took a step back, waving her inside.

"That's why I'm paying a small fortune to that lady lawyer to keep me out of jail."

It would be worth rebuilding that nest egg if this all went away. "What brings you by?"

Her lips twitched at my attempt to change the subject.

"I came because I heard you did something really stupid. You broke up with Slayer."

I folded my arms defensively, unsure if she was here to threaten me or sympathize. Did I even want Peaches to intervene?

"Well your sources are wrong because I didn't break up with him. *He* walked away from *me*."

He'd done it easily, too, and me, lovesick idiot that I was, I was still shocked that he had.

"Is that all?"

"No, actually." Peaches looked surprised, but I didn't care either way. It was better to know now that I'd chosen the wrong man again. My man-picker was broken.

"I'm here for a different reason, but I wanted to get the goods on you and Slayer first. I've got some dirt."

I frowned. "I'm not in the market for dirt, Peaches. I don't have a garden or a green thumb."

"Not that kind of dirt, weirdo. Got something to eat? I'm starved."

The woman must have had too much coffee this morning because I was having a hard time keeping up with her hairpin conversational turns.

"Sure. Come on." She followed me into the kitchen and without shame, I pulled a half eaten pizza from the oven, still in its box.

"What kind of dirt are we talking?"

I piled the pizza on two plates and arranged buffalo nuggets on a third. I brought them to the table and rushed back to the kitchen for a beer for Peaches since mine was still half full.

"You have soda or water?" she asked, her gaze firmly focused on the black laptop she'd taken out of a badass looking metal case.

"Feeling weird lately, and I don't know if it's a bug or a baby yet."

"Well, you're in luck, because one of my favorite things about Texas is sweet tea."

I poured her a tall glass and waited for her to tell me why she was at my house.

"That's damn good," she said and smacked her lips before killing off one slice of pizza and half of another.

"Congratulations," I said instead of anything sarcastic or snarky.

Still, she narrowed her gaze at me. "Thanks. Smartass."

Her greasy fingers flew over the keyboard, and then she turned back to me.

"The dirt is on McAllister and it's good."

"But?"

Peaches sighed and pulled the flash drive out and held it out to me.

"But I need you not to look at it. Just give it to your lawyer."

I reached for the little pink drive, but Peaches held it back.

"Seriously," she said, narrowing her eyes to show she meant business. "Promise."

I threw up my hands. "Fine, I promise. Why?"

"I know how guys like him operate. He'll say you planted it, or created it, or manipulated it somehow. Trust me that this is concrete evidence to keep you out of prison. Just let the high-priced lawyer do her thing. In court."

I felt like I was missing a part of the puzzle, but Peaches didn't have to help me, yet here she was.

"Okay thanks."

I was desperate for anything that would maintain my freedom, so I agreed like a kid greedy for an ice cream in exchange for clearing the table.

"But, why?"

"You don't trust me?"

I laughed. "I don't *not* trust you, but I am curious why you're going above and beyond."

"Besides the fact that I'm addicted to watching Slayer fall in love and to *be* in love? And, I like you. I think you're good people."

"You don't even know me."

"Not really, but I do. You're a strong chick like me. Like Annabelle. The other girls are strong but in a different way. I think you and me could be friends."

I accepted that answer because I could use more friends who weren't just interested in fucking the guys in my MC. "Okay."

She laughed. "Damn, and I had a whole speech ready about how you helped me keep my baby girl and how that makes you family."

I frowned. "What?"

"Maisie's so called father? Rocco?"

"Oh, that? Screw that dick, I was happy to do it."

"Exactly. My family means everything to me, Chance, and now you're part of that, whether you want it or not. I got your back."

She dropped the pink drive on the table and scooped up her plate and headed for the kitchen.

I picked up the flash drive and weighed in my hand. Was this my ticket out of jail? "Thanks," I said quietly.

"Anytime," she said with a warm smile as she washed her plate and dried her hands. Then she turned to me. "Now that this shit show is off your plate, maybe you can pull your head out of your ass and fix things with Slayer."

I laughed and walked her to the door.

"Is this what it's like to have real girlfriends? Because I gotta say, I'm not a fan."

Peaches' laugh came out deep and throaty, full-bodied.

"Hell, yeah. We're loud and crazy and chaos follows us wherever wc go. We get all up in each other's business, and sometimes we come to blows over it. But we're always there for each other when the shit hits the fan, which it inevitably does. Always."

She rolled her eyes playfully and pulled me in for a hug.

"Besides, this whole Counsel thing was your idea."

Damn, she was right. "What was I thinking?"

Peaches laughed and shook her head, wild copper curls twisting on the breeze.

"You were thinking about that dick," she laughed. "See you soon."

I didn't know if things could be fixed with Slayer, but I knew that if there was a chance, I'd take it.

After tomorrow's hearing.

Chapter Thirty-Three

Slayer

I showed up at the courthouse early, hoping I might be able to get a few moments alone with Chance before the official proceedings began. According to Peaches, this was just a hearing to determine if there was enough evidence to go to trial, not the start of her trial. No matter what, Chance was coming home today.

She just wasn't coming home with me.

And that pissed me off.

But I owed her an apology for walking away, for not being a man and explaining myself better. That pissed-off, immature prick from the party wasn't me.

Judging by the size of the crowd that had gathered today, I might have a hard time prying her away from her supporters. That's if she was even willing to talk to me. Something I doubted, especially today. All the wives and girlfriends of the Reckless Bastards came to support Chance, along with the Ladies of Buckthorn. The Bastards and the Lords had also gathered on the courthouse steps.

But where was Chance?

Finally, less than five minutes before the hearing began, she stepped from the passenger side of a sleek red sedan and joined her lawyer on the sidewalk. Together, they walked up the steps looking competent and badass. Who'd want to fuck with those two women? Chance had her game face on, but not even the sharp black suit could hide the fear and worry in her eyes.

I wanted to wrap my arms around her, tell her it would all turn out okay in the end. But I honestly didn't know. I didn't know if she'd even welcome my arms around her, and I wasn't sure it *would* turn out okay. One thing for sure, I wouldn't lie to her.

It took some time for everyone to find a seat in the courtroom since the MCs and their women took up all the rows behind Chance and her lawyer. That left Leon's brother and the few members of the press that had shown up to play musical chairs behind the prosecutor. It was a small courtroom with just eight benches, just enough to let the judge see Chance wasn't alone.

The gray-haired judge shuffled out and took his seat, banging the gavel and bringing the room to complete silence.

"All right let's get this show on the road. Anything new?"

His blue gaze bounced from McAllister to Monica, who stood and addressed the court.

"Yes, Your Honor. Some new evidence has recently come to light that will make us all rethink the prosecution of Ella Mae Ambrose."

"Objection, Your Honor! This is not the time or the place to present new evidence." McAllister was red in the face, but more than that, he looked worried. Maybe even a little scared.

Monica's perfectly sculpted eyebrows arched in amusement.

"If not now, during the preliminary hearing, when should we present evidence that will clear my client?"

He sputtered, choking on his words before turning back to the judge. "This is highly inappropriate, Your Honor."

"It just might be," Monica began again. "But I plead with you to hear the evidence and decide for yourself. If it's a waste of time, find me in contempt."

Monica was more than confident; she was arrogant but it seemed like the judge was buying it.

Chance's gaze hadn't moved further right than Monica or further left than the judge, not bothering to cast a grateful look to anyone behind her. Me especially.

"And if I find it isn't a waste of time, Miss Stevenson?"

"Then I'll file a motion to dismiss and drop the charges. With prejudice."

The last two words were aimed at McAllister, who suddenly looked very uneasy.

Still, Chance was stoic, damn near emotionless as she sat there listening to other people argue and decide her fate. I couldn't take my eyes off of her as the lawyers threw barbs back and forth, the fierce expression on her face said she'd fight like hell for her freedom.

And didn't that just make me feel like a real asshole, once more, for walking away from a woman like Chance? But I wasn't wrong, I knew that. Why couldn't she see that *she* was what I needed? The only thing I wanted in this world was her right by my side. Even if she ended up in jail, I wouldn't stop trying to free her by any means necessary.

Gunnar elbowed me from the right and Cruz from the left. "You even listening, fucker?"

I shook my head because I hadn't been listening. I was too busy watching Chance, looking for any sign that she was all right. But the courtroom doors flew open and two bailiffs entered, rolling a big ass audio visual cart. In just a few minutes it was all set up, and Monica stood in front of the cart and dramatically pressed a button that filled the courtroom with a familiar voice.

"Don't worry about it. I deleted the footage from the drive thing those dumb fuckers gave us at that sex club."

McAllister laughed out loud and, I shit you not, it was a perfect imitation of an evil villain's laugh.

"So many familiar faces on that video, I couldn't actually delete it, not when that one night of footage will come in handy in the future. Especially for my career."

It wasn't clear exactly who McAllister was talking to, but his own words were damning enough.

"Why not just use the footage for blackmail and leave the girl alone?"

The voice was male, but that's all I could make out with the static and the sound of loud music in the background.

"No way. That biker bitch is going down. The dead guy's brother told me how she played him, a

veteran for fuck's sake. His family has some clout in Austin and putting her behind bars will make them ever so grateful."

The fucker changed to his best southern accent, then laughed and laughed for a full minute at the end of the call. Monica played every second of the tape.

McAllister's face turned pale and sweaty as the creeping sensation of being up shit creek without a paddle sank in.

"I'd like to request a brief recess, Your Honor," he managed to stammer out despite the judge's glare.

"Request denied," the judge spat out as he banged his gavel. "Who here in this courtroom works for Mr. McAllister?"

A young redhead in a bow tie struggled to his feet and raised his hand. "Wesley Parrish, Judge. First year attorney."

"Congratulations, son. You are ordered to produce this audio file to the court by the end of the day. You can manage that?"

"Absolutely, Your Honor. To your office or the Clerk's?"

"Directly to me, Mr. Parrish. And hurry."

WILD

The kid took off as if his own future hung in the balance. The rest of us held our breath.

And waited.

Two hours later it was all over; Chance was in the clear.

Free. Charges dismissed.

Now there was nothing else in our way.

Nothing but us.

Chapter Thirty-Four

Ella Mae

Free. I was free, and it felt damn good. Really damn good. Unfortunately, it didn't feel as good as it should have. Good enough, though, that I had a smile on my face as my family surrounded me on the steps of the courthouse. They pulled me in for so many hugs and kisses, fist bumps, and smiles that I was dizzy.

"How does it feel, Chance, to know you won't have to eat muff for the next fifteen years?"

Leave it to Brick to get down to what really mattered.

I threw my head back and laughed as my club surrounded me, ignoring the big ache behind my chest.

"I'm only sad that now you'll only have your memory of the last time a woman touched your wiener to help you get off. I would've taken one for the team but now...I don't have to."

"Aw, Chance." Brick tossed his hands up in the air, but all the Lords of Buckthorn groaned. I laughed again at my winning streak when it comes to grossing the guys out.

"What? You asked for it?"

"Yeah, yeah," Curt said as he grabbed me around the shoulders.

"Come on, let's get outta here. Too many cops are making me itch."

I elbowed him in the side and laughed.

"That might be the waitress you spent last night with."

I stopped joking and looked around, realizing I hadn't seen Monica since thanking her for taking McAllister down. All the way *down*.

"Shit. My ride is gone."

"Don't worry Chance. We got you." Brick handed me a duffel bag, with my jeans, a t-shirt and my favorite motorcycle boots.

I was touched down to my core. My thanks choked in my throat, so I wrapped both men in big hugs I knew they would hate and darted off to the nearest bathroom before I did something really stupid, like start crying.

When I came back in my own clothes, I felt like a new woman.

A free woman.

WILD

Brick motioned me over. "You're ridin' with me. Come on."

I hopped on the back of Brick's bike and held on tight, closing my eyes as the wind whipped all around me. I could feel the bike eating up the road, and I relished that feel, especially since just this morning I wasn't sure I'd ever feel this alive again.

The biked slowed too soon, and I opened my eyes with a frown.

"Why are we stopping?"

It was a ridiculous question when I recognized the path exactly, but still I waited for an answer over the roar of the engine.

"We're heading to Hardtail Ranch. Where else?"

"Maybe our own clubhouse? Just an idea."

Anywhere but the damn backyard where it all happened. But that was on me, I should have realized. The Reckless Bastards and their women had all shown up to support me, and I appreciated it, even though I hadn't said as much.

Brick stopped his bike near the gleaming big white house and looked over as shoulder to prompt me to get off the damn bike.

"Any day now, Chance."

"I guess they're all in there, huh?"

"Yep. Waiting on you. The woman of the hour."

I smiled at his gruffly spoken sweet words. I swung my leg off the bike.

"You say the sweetest things, Brick."

"Yep, that's me. Sweet as fucking pie."

He was rough and gruff, but Brick was the marshmallow of the bunch.

"Seriously, I'm glad as fuck you're not going to prison. I don't want the number two spot. I'm happy where I am."

"Damn, and I thought it's 'cause you'd miss me too much."

"That too," he said, lips kicking up into a lopsided grin. "Ready?"

"No, but when has that ever stopped me?"

I held the grin, more for my sake than Brick's and sucked in a deep breath, letting it out slowly as I watched Brick climb the steps that led to the Reckless Bastards.

To one Reckless Bastard in general.

Slayer.

Chapter Thirty-Five

Slayer

I was happy as hell that Chance was free and wouldn't spend any more time behind bars than she already had, but I wasn't in the mood for a fucking party. I wanted to grab Chance and toss her leggy ass over my shoulder and carry her home where she would have no choice but to listen to me.

But Chance wasn't here, not yet. I saw Curt, Brick, and a few of the other Lords walk out of the big house. The big man stood at the top of the steps with one hand shoved in his pocket, taking in the party as a whole. It was an odd mix, both MCs mingling and laughing and drinking together like we'd been part of this fucking Counsel for years rather than weeks.

Cruz came up behind me. "Dude, it's a party. Stop glaring at everybody before someone takes it the wrong way." He meant it as a joke, casting a wary look over at Curt talking tattoos with Hennessy.

"I can take anyone here. Including you," I told him seriously.

Cruz just laughed. And laughed. It was pretty damn obnoxious, actually. "You wish. One knee kick and you'd go down."

"Don't need my legs to make you submit in less than fifteen seconds. Wanna test that theory?"

Cruz took a step back and stared at me like he was trying to figure out what the hell was wrong with me.

"You'd really rather fight me than go fight for your woman?"

I sighed at his words. "Might not be anything left to fight for."

"Bullshit. You were wrong. You think you weren't, but you were. Hell, you *are* wrong, so just fucking apologize. Tell her you love her and promise to do better every day you're together."

Was I wrong, though? "I shouldn't have walked away."

"No, you shouldn't have. Asshole. You also shouldn't have forced her to decide on a future that wasn't a possibility. Shit man, that fucking lawyer was gonna lock her up knowing she was innocent!"

He was right. It was even worse now, after sitting through the hearing, and now Chance was here. She stood in the same spot Brick had just vacated, one hand shoved in her back pocket and the other holding an icy cocktail.

"I know. I'm working on it."

"Work fast, man. Ford has a brand new patch, and I'm sure he wouldn't mind a fine woman like Chance."

"Fuck you. Not funny."

Cruz laughed and clapped me on the back. "A little funny. I'm going to dance with my woman. Maybe I'll see you out there. Maybe not," he called over his shoulder with a laugh.

The coast was clear. It was now or never.

I chose now.

Walking across the grass, I met Chance at the bottom of the steps. I smiled and said, "Hey."

"Hey," she replied quietly. It wasn't quite what I hoped for, but she hadn't walked away.

"Congratulations."

Her smile flashed a little brighter this time, and she ducked her head in a shy motion that was so unlike her, I reached my hand out to her and let a few tendrils of hair brush against my fingertips.

"Thanks. It feels good to have that behind me. Thank you for your support."

I shrugged. "Where else would I be?"

Her smile dimmed. "You walked away from me, Slayer. You could be anywhere else."

I nodded for her to follow me, and Chance's long legs fell into step beside me. We walked around the big house toward the big field where we sometimes kept the cattle.

"I'm sorry for walking away. I shouldn't have done it. I was pissed off. Really pissed off."

I raked a hand through my head and let out a breath.

"This whole Counsel thing was your idea and you were walking away. From us. Damn right I was pissed."

I wish I could make her see but talking about it pissed me off all over again.

"I wasn't walking away, Slayer. I was fighting for my life. My freedom!"

"I know. I do, I really do know that, Chance. But dammit, I love you. I would wait for you."

She shook her head, ignoring the wisps of hair the breeze kept picking up and blowing across her face.

"I couldn't ask you to do that and I wouldn't. Not ever. You're too vibrant and too lively to be stuck waiting on someday, and I love you too much to condemn you to that life."

I love you too much. Those words brought a smile to my face.

My voice cracked when I said, "You do?"

She nodded. "Luckily, prison is no longer on my ten-year-plan."

I took a step forward and leaned in, twirling a lock of her hair around my finger.

"What, or *who* is in those plans?"

"I don't know, Slayer. I love you, and that hasn't changed, but damn, we're fucked up. Both of us, me more than you. And now our MCs are working together, and we'll be fighting side by side. How will this work?"

I could tell by her expression she was serious. That she actually believed this.

"It'll work because we'll make it work. You are one stubborn woman, and I'm determined as hell."

Those words sparked her anger, and she folded her arms across her chest, taking a step back.

"Come again?"

"You heard me, but let's not worry about all that," I told her with an easy smile. "I love you Chance. I fucking love the hell out of you, and you keep looking for reasons why this can't work. Won't work."

The air rushed out of my lungs on those words and I looked at her, stared really. Waiting.

"That's because I'm scared of how good we are together, and I'm more scared of losing that. Can't you understand that?"

Hell, yeah. Her words took all the fight out of me, and I felt my shoulders fall in defeat.

"I do understand it, more than you know. I'm fucking terrified too, but I'm more terrified of living without you. Of not giving this thing a real shot and missing out on something pretty fucking great."

Her smile came slowly, so damn slowly my fingers twitched in eagerness to hear what she would say next.

"I love you, too, Slayer, and I really want this to work out. Really."

"Christ, woman, was that so hard?"

Just like that her expression changed, darkened, and intensified as her hand landed on my chest and slowly slid down to the waistband of my pants.

"I don't know Slayer, *is it?* Hard?"

WILD

"Fuckin' tease," I growled and nipped her ear. And when she turned with a shocked laugh, I stole the kiss I'd been dreaming about for days. The kiss I thought I might never get to experience again. Right now I had Chance in my arms. Life was good. She moaned when I pulled back from the kiss with a smile.

"Your place or mine?"

"Well since yours is much closer, I think that question answers itself."

She leaned in again and pressed her body and those lush lips against mine, and I felt like I'd died and gone to heaven.

And then I took Chance home and took us both to heaven.

Three times.

Epilogue

Chance ~ 6 weeks later

How could my life change so much in six weeks? That was the first thought I had as my eyes opened and then shut right away because neither Slayer nor me had thought to close the blinds before we attacked each other. Ripped off each other's clothes and went at it like two horny twenty-one-year olds on Spring Break. The second thought I had? How could one body ache so much from two simple orgasms? Three if you counted the one that had started it all downstairs in the kitchen.

I totally counted it.

But now, in bed beside Slayer, the heat of his big body making up for the fact that he was a blanket hog, a third thought crossed my mind.

It was time.

It was something I'd been avoiding for weeks, maybe close to a month if I was being honest with myself. I swung my legs over the bed and cast one final look over my shoulder at Slayer's sleeping form before walking on screaming thigh muscles to the bathroom. Once inside, I flipped on the shower and then locked the door.

Steps one and two complete.

Next, I filled the cup beside the sink with cold water and drank it until my belly was uncomfortably full. Dangerously full, at least it might have been if I wasn't in the bathroom. And on a mission.

Five minutes later, all five missions were laid out on the counter, each one of them saying a different variation of the same thing. I was pregnant. Knocked up. With child. Up thee duff. I was having a baby. With a biker.

Not just any old biker, but *my* big bearded biker with a filthy mouth and a heart of gold. I was having Slayer's baby, and now I just needed to tell him.

It was too soon; I knew that. We'd barely been living together for a month that we could bump to seven weeks if you really wanted to, but it was still too soon. It was either going to be another reason to celebrate, which we've had plenty of lately, or it was another reason to toss my cookies. Both were real and distinctive possibilities, but I was too overwhelmed to decide which was more likely.

How were we having a baby after less than a year of dating and living together? I stepped into the still running shower and stayed there until the hot water ran lukewarm.

"Chance? Everything all right in there?" Slayer's big fist landed on the door after he turned the knob and found it locked. "Chance?"

I'd just stepped from the shower and reached over to open the door before I grabbed a towel.

"What's up?"

He frowned, his face still showing sleep lines from the pillowcase and bedding. "Why is the door locked?"

I stepped in close and put my hands to his chest, feeling the wild thudding of his heart as I pushed up to kiss him, long and slow. It was hot and sweet, and instantly, my body was ready for more.

Not yet.

"I just needed some privacy, that's all."

He took a step back and gave me a quizzical look, which I found hella sexy. I tried to keep my focus on his handsome face, not his gorgeous chest, or ink covered skin.

"Privacy? From me?"

"Not *from* you, Slayer. Just privacy. Needed to process some things, that's all."

I wrapped the towel around my body and went to the vanity.

"We good?"

I hated that he felt the need to ask that question. The last thing I had in mind was to put some kind of obstacle between us.

"We're good. Better than good, in fact."

I squeezed a dollop of moisturizer on my hand and took my time rubbing it into my skin.

"That is if you consider having a baby a good thing."

I wasn't even sure how I felt about this baby and all the changes it would require, but I was happy I was doing it with Slayer.

"Were having a baby?"

His eyes lit up and his smile was a big as Texas. Maybe he did think having a baby is a good thing.

I turned and folded my arms. "Yes, a baby."

"Maybe you'll say yes the next time I ask you to be my wife? How do you feel about it?"

I shrugged. "Processing. I guess I'm in shock."

That was the truth. A baby was the last thing I expected.

"I figured the MC would be my life, that I'd be the fun auntie to all the kids the guys would have. But now

WILD

that I know we've got our own little rider in here? Shit Slayer, I'm pretty damn stoked about it."

And then I was in Slayer's big tattooed arms, and he was holding me tight like he never wanted to let me go. And it felt damn good, because I didn't plan on going anywhere for a really long time.

"Me too," he growled into my hair and squeezed just a little tighter.

"We're having a baby."

Slayer's smile was so bright, I had to shield my eyes as he grabbed my other hand and pulled me out of the bathroom. He dug in my lingerie drawer, yanking out different colors of silk and lace and tulle until he found what he was looking for, and then Slayer was headed my way once again.

And dropping down on one knee, like a fucking prince!

"Ella Mae."

He laughed at the glare I sent him.

"Chance. Babe. Love of my fucking life, whatever you want me to call you. You are my heart and my soul. You woke me up when I didn't even know I was sleeping, barely living aside from the MC. You've got a potty mouth, a body built for sin, and the most

345

spectacular laugh I have ever heard in my whole damn life."

The love shining back at me from his eyes was almost more than I could bear, except it was exactly the look I'd been waiting for my whole life.

"Chance," he said, "we've got a strange and probably fucked up road ahead of us, but I can't think of another badass I want to have at my side. What do you say?"

I sucked in a breath at his words, but when Slayer slid the platinum band with black and white diamonds wrapped into an infinity symbol, I felt my knees go weak. Actual weak knees, *and* I felt a tear sliding down my cheek. I looked at the ring and then at the man who had turned my whole world upside down. I could feel my smile beaming when I blurted out, "I say yes. Hell, yes, Slayer. I'll take this wild fucked up ride with you."

"By my side," he said with a smile.

"For all of the time we have left," I told him honestly because that's how long I wanted to live this life with this man.

"Damn straight," he shot back with a sexy, filthy grin I felt all the way down to my toes.

By the time the afternoon rolled around, Slayer and I had showered again and put on clothes so we could make our way over to the big house to share our good news.

"It's strange, feeling so happy. Isn't it?"

"Hell, no," Slayer said and dropped a kiss to my forehead. "I deserve it, dammit, and so do you. It took us too long to find each other. We're due for all the happy we can stand."

"Amen, babe."

His lips curled into a smile at my words. "Baby. We're having a baby!" And then he hugged me and twirled me around.

"Eww, get a room." Maisie stomped out of the back door and down the porch steps, more attitude than a pre-teen girl should have. "There are *kids* around here. Apparently."

I looked back at my fiancé with raised eyebrows. "See what we have to look forward to?"

He shook his head and grabbed Maisie by the arm. "What's up kiddo?"

"It's not fair, Uncle Slayer! All the guys are going to Vegas *and* getting tattoos from Uncle Tate, and I haven't seen him in for*ever* and Gunnar won't let me go! My life sucks!"

She stomped off just as Gunnar slammed the back door open.

"Maisie, you're too young!"

"Not listening," she called out and kept on walking until she was at her favorite spot on the ranch, the horse paddock.

"What's going on?" Slayer posed the question to Gunnar who looked like he'd rather be anywhere than fighting with his kid.

"Ford wants his Reckless Bastards' tat now, and he's earned it. Shit, we kept him as a prospect for too long, but I can't go to Vegas and now Saint and Hazel are in on the fucking adventure."

"Tats?" Slayer looked like he was ready to fuel up our bikes at that on word.

"Don't even think about it," Gunnar warned, but Slayer's smile was already aimed at me.

"We could get married in Vegas," he said and wiggled his eyebrows. Dammit, it was tempting.

"No bridal shower. No dress fittings. Cake tastings."

"Hell, Slayer, I couldn't love you more if I tried. But we're not going."

Damnit. Who could resist a man that eager to make me his wife? A man who would hop on his bike to Vegas just to save me from a century of wedding traditions.

He smiled and pressed his forehead to mine. "You go, I go."

It was so tempting. "We're not going. I'm pregnant, remember? And the Lords?"

"But you're mine now, baby."

I kissed him on the cheek and whispered, "And I always will be."

T H E   E N D

Acknowledgements

Thank you so much for making my books a success! I appreciate all of you! Thanks to all of my beta readers, street teamers, ARC readers and Facebook fans. Y'all are THE BEST!

And a huge very special thanks to Jessie! I'm such a *hot mess, but without your keen sense of organization and skills, I'd be a burny fiery inferno of hot mess!! Thank you!

And a very special thanks to my editors (who sometimes have to work all through the night! *See HOT MESS above!) Thank you for making my words make sense.

Copyright © 2020 KB Winters and BookBoyfriends Publishing Inc

KB WINTERS

About The Author

KB Winters is a Wall Street Journal and USA Today Bestselling Author of steamy hot books about Bikers, Billionaires, Bad Boys and Badass Military Men. Just the way you like them. She has an addiction to caffeine, tattoos and hard-bodied alpha males. The men in her books are very sexy, protective and sometimes bossy, her ladies are...well...*bossier*!

Living in sunny Southern California, with her amazing man and fur babies, this embarrassingly hopeless romantic writes every chance she gets!

You can reach KB at Facebook.com/kbwintersauthor and at kbwintersauthor@gmail.com

Copyright © 2020 KB Winters and BookBoyfriends Publishing Inc

Printed in Great Britain
by Amazon